South American
Wonder Tales

SOUTH AMERICAN WONDER TALES

by Frances Carpenter

illustrated by Ralph Creasman

Follett Publishing Company
Chicago F *New York*

Standard Book Number 695-48214-9 Titan binding
Standard Book Number 695-88214-7 Trade binding

Library of Congress Card Number: 69-10250

First Printing D

ABOUT THESE WONDER TALES

DURING my recent journeys to the great South American continent, I have visited almost all the lands from which have come the folktales in this book. As I traveled from its northern Caribbean shores to its southern tip at Cape Horn, I have been constantly impressed by the likeness of the places and people of today with those found in the pages of this book.

In the hot northern regions I have watched Indians like Tio and his "Honeybee Bride," leap about in wild fire-dances. I have seen native huts in jungle clearings like that in the story of "The-Pot-That-Cooked-by-Itself." In the magnificent ruins of the Incas of Peru, I could easily imagine the young shepherd, Allpa, eloping with his beloved Sun Princess under the protection of his magic poncho.

Cruising along the muddy northern rivers, their jungle-clad banks seemed believable homes for crocodiles and giant snakes, for strange birds and rare butterflies. At any moment, I expected to see a jabuty or a jaguar, a paca or an emerald-green beetle.

In the great South American cities I found houses as fine as the hacienda in the tale of "The Little Black Book of Magic"; and I met pretty girls quite as clever as Carmelita who outwitted the proud Spanish Governor.

Folktales such as these tell us much about the South America of today. Its rivers still run through jungle tangles. Hot northern winds and cool breezes from the south still blow across the vast grasslands. Its mountains raise their heads thousands upon thousands of feet into the air, just as they did in the long ago. The ways of many modern South Americans are different, but for others their daily life is much the same as it was for the people found in these tales.

Frances Carpenter

CONTENTS

South American
Wonder Tales

THE GREAT BIRD IN THE CAROB TREE

A GIANT BIRD whose wings reached from one end of the sky to the other, is the villain of this story. And a courageous young Indian named Tópac, may be called its hero. Not less important, however, is a carob tree with shining green leaves.

Good luck is found in the shade of a carob tree. The Indians of the western highlands of South America say this is so. And they should know. For it was in their part of the land that a carob tree saved their forefathers from dying of thirst.

It happened long, long ago when there came a hot summer such as never was known, before or since. For days without end, the rain did not fall. Without any break, the sun sent its fierce burning rays down upon the green plains, the broad grass lands which in Argentina are called the pampas.

The pampas turned first yellow, then brown for lack of water. The little brooks ran no more. Even the big streams and lakes dried in their beds. The plants drooped their heads, lower and lower. At last their leaves were so dry that they crumbled to powder.

"Our children cry. Our llamas die of hunger and thirst." The people shook their heads sadly as they looked at their thin pant-

11

ing beasts. Next to their children their little camel-like llamas were more important than anything else in their world.

This was in the times before the Spanish conquerors came to America from across the wide ocean, bringing with them their horses, cattle, and sheep. For the Indians, their llamas took the place of all three of these useful animals. They carried their loads. Their meat was good to eat, and their hides provided leather. The wool off their backs, like that of sheep, was made into thread and woven into cloth.

In the great heat and drought, without green grass or water, the llamas were almost too weak to stand up. Ostriches could no longer run fast, nor could they kick out at their enemies. Armadillos could not bear to stay in their burrows in the burning earth. By day as well as by night, they crept about on their short legs in search of a drink.

"Somehow, somewhere we must find water for ourselves and our beasts," the poor people said to each other. And they drove their llamas hither and yon over the dry land.

"There! Look! There is water over there." One day a young herdboy pointed excitedly to a shining spot in the distance.

But his elders shook their heads. "That is not water, *niño*," they said sadly. "That is only a trick played by the gods. When we reach that place, we shall find nothing but more dry yellow grass."

And that was how it was. On certain days on the pampas, when the air was very hot and very dry, pools of shining blue appeared in places where no water ever is found. Such a sight is known as a mirage. It is the hot air which acts like a mirror and reflects bits of the blue sky.

12

Things went from bad to worse. The pampas became a desert from one end to the other.

At last, one of the young Indians cried to the others, "There must be a reason why the rain does not come. The gods must have forgotten us. I will go seek the cause of their anger. And I will not come back until I have found out what we must do to bring the rain down from out of the clouds."

This bold young man, whose name was Tópac, set out across the broad plain. It was a hot journey. Nowhere did he find a tree to shade him from the sun. He walked and he walked. And finally he came to a dry riverbed.

"Tell me, O River," he asked, "Why are you dry? Why have you no water for my poor thirsty throat?"

Strange things happened in those long ago times. Spirits of rivers, and trees, and even animals talked. So Tópac, the young Indian, was in no way surprised when a voice came out of the dry riverbed to answer him.

"Alas, good young man," it said, "I have no water because the Mother-of-Storms sends me no rain. She must be asleep. She must have forgotten this part of the land."

As he went on his way, Tópac looked to the south. It was from that direction that Pampero, the cool South Wind, so often brought rain. But he felt on his cheeks only the burning breath of the wind that swept down from the Equator, far to the north.

"Ah, North Wind," Tópac cried, "where is your brother, Pampero? Why does he not come to us? Why does he not bring us the rain we need so very much?"

The North Wind replied brusquely, "No doubt Pampero sleeps. No doubt he has forgotten this part of the land." Then he rushed

13

away, blowing up clouds of dry dust from off the parched earth.

Next Tópac turned his face to the heavens. He lifted his arms high and sent up prayers to the gods.

"O, Giver-of-all-Life, have pity upon us!" he prayed to the sun. "Hide your fiery face behind clouds! Give us rest from your heat!" But no cloud appeared in the sky.

"O, Pacha-Mama," now he prayed to the Earth-Mother, "wake from your slumber. Send water into your springs and your wells. Save us, Pacha-Mama. Your children are dying of thirst." But again no help came.

"O, Mother-of-Storms!" he cried. You see, he did not omit any of the powerful gods in whom his people believed. "Have you indeed forgotten us, Mother-of-Storms? Come! Bring us rain! Bring us rain!"

But none of the gods answered his prayers. The sun burned as bright, the land was as dry as before.

Poor Tópac was too weary to go any farther. Luckily, just then he came to a carob tree. The broad Argentine pampas were almost without trees, and this was the first which Tópac had found in his wandering. With a sigh of relief, he threw himself down to rest in its cool shade.

"Wonder of wonders!" he said to himself as he raised his eyes, "the leaves of this carob tree are still fresh and green."

Then he remembered that this kind of tree had roots which went down deep, deep into the earth where they found water pockets under the ground, well hidden from the heat of the sun.

"Ah, Carob Tree," he cried out, "what a good friend you are! In all this dry land, you alone help the traveler. Tell me, what have my people done that we should have to suffer so much?

14

I have called upon Pacha-Mama. I have prayed to the sun and the Mother-of-Storms. But they do not answer."

"Good youth," the voice came out of the Carob Tree. "No blame is yours. The cause of your trouble is that the gods are asleep. They truly have forgotten this part of the land.

"But no blame is theirs either. They cannot see these broad pampas. The wicked Great Bird from the Underworld hides it from their sight."

"The Great Bird from the Underworld!" Tópac repeated the words. He never had heard of such a thing.

"Such a great bird, my friend, as has never before been seen in this land. Its wings are so large that they reach from one end of the sky to the other. When the Great Bird circles above the pampas, halfway between these grassy plains and the heavens, his wings hide the whole earth from the gods. How should they remember to care for the people whom they cannot see?"

Tópac wondered still more. "What, then, shall we do?" he asked in great distress.

"The Great Bird must be driven away. His wicked game must be stopped. The gods must be awakened and reminded of their duty to man." The voice from the Carob Tree sounded as if this might be possible.

"Where can the Great Bird be found?" Tópac cried. "Can a man kill it? What must I do to drive it away?"

"No man can kill the Great Bird," came the answer from the rustling green leaves. "But many men, many together—yes, many might frighten the wicked bird so that it would go away by itself.

"Every evening, the Great Bird comes to my branches for shelter. Upon my highest limb it sleeps until the sun lights the

15

skies once again. Then it flies out to circle above the earth."

"Gather your brothers and sisters here around my trunk when the moon shines," said the voice from the Carob Tree. "Make noise! Oh, make noise so loud that the gods in the sky must awake! Make noise so awesome that the Great Bird will be frightened away!"

Of course, Tópac lost no time in calling his people to gather under the Carob Tree. As soon as the moon rose, they beat upon drums. They shrieked and they screamed. They filled the air with a din that shook the earth, and rose high into the heavens.

Suddenly there was a movement in the branches of the Carob Tree. Its top swayed this way and that. It seemed almost as if it would bend down to the ground.

Then, out of the treetop, the Great Bird rose into the air. Up, up, and up it flew, until the bright moon was hidden by its enormous wings.

"Louder! Now louder!" Tópac shouted with all his might. And the drums and the screams of the crowd increased.

"The Great Bird is gone!" Tópac cried. And the people all echoed his words, "The Great Bird is gone!"

They sent songs up to Heaven calling again on Pacha-Mama, the Earth-Mother. They prayed again to Pampero, the South Wind, and to the Mother-of-Storms. They danced and they shouted and beat on their drums so as surely to waken these gods.

At last Tópac gave a cry.

"Look! There in the south! A cloud rises. It spreads. Pampero is coming."

Hardly were the words spoken, when the whole sky grew dark. Gray clouds veiled the moon. Thunder rolled in the distance.

16

Then the rain came! The people rushed out from under the Carob Tree. They held their mouths open wide to wet their dry swollen tongues. The animals lapped up the water that gathered in pools in the hard-baked earth.

Like their cousins the camels, llamas can go a long time without water. But this summer had been far too long for them. They leaped for joy when they tasted sweet water once more.

People hugged each other in delight as they sniffed the delicious, damp air. Going back to the shelter of the Carob Tree, they watched the torrents of rain soak the dry thirsty earth.

Ever since that day, the Indians of the western pampas have honored the carob tree. In parts of the land, even now, they make feasts under its branches. On a moonlight night at the harvest time, they gather to sing and to dance and beat upon drums.

When the festival is over, they take away baskets of the red-yellow pods. The soft pulp of the pods makes a good drink. Dried carob beans can be pounded into flour for porridge and cakes.

Although it takes a carob tree a long time to grow, some people plant its seeds beside their low ranch homes. They are sure that the trees, which will eventually give them shade, will bring them good luck as well.

THE CROCODILE'S DAUGHTER

In THE BEGINNING, the world was a good place, a different place, and a far better place than it is today. Flowers bloomed the year round. Fruit hung on the trees in winter as well as in summer and fall. The rivers were calm, even where they flowed over high rocks and cliffs. The rains always fell softly. The sun was never too hot.

In those times the animals were friendly with one another. The small armadillo never had to roll itself up inside its hard shell for fear the larger creatures would harm it. The timid agouty, no bigger than a rabbit, was not afraid to play with a jaguar's tail. There was no poison in the bite of any snake. And a turtle could lay her eggs on the land without fear they would be eaten.

At first, there were no men and no women at all on the earth, no boys and no girls, so the old story says. When the Maker-of-All-Things looked down from the sky, he found his earth good. And he said to himself, "There should be people. There should be men and women, and boys and girls to enjoy this pleasant world I have made."

So he came down to the earth.

18

As he walked through the forest along the seashore, the first creature he met was a huge crocodile of the kind called a cayman. And it was this one he chose to be the father of man.

"Your children, O Crocodile, shall grow into people. They shall become men and women. They shall live in my world and enjoy all the good things I have made." This is what the Maker-of-All-Things said to the cayman.

So it happened. At least it did in the South American legend. The crocodile's daughters were all good to look at. But the sons were of two sorts. Some were very handsome. Others were ugly, with the heads of crocodiles.

Now the handsome ones did not like to look at their ugly brothers. And the ugly ones were jealous of their brothers' handsome human faces. So they decided to separate. The ugly ones went to one part of the world. The handsome ones traveled far in the opposite direction. And all took their wives with them.

The sun rose and set, and rose and set. Years went by. In the part of the world where the handsome men lived, in one of the tribes, there was a certain young man whose name was almost too long to pronounce. It began with Maco—and we may as well let it go at that.

Maco was a fine fellow. He stood straight and strong. His face was like that of a god. And when he moved he had the grace of a jaguar. No other in his tribe was so clever as this young man. When there was a clay pot to be shaped or a basket to be woven, his people said "We'll take it to Maco. He'll know how the task should be done."

The good youth lived with his mother in a hut on the seashore. Like her son, the old woman was well thought of in the tribe.

19

To her, the other women came for help in making their meal out of the manioc roots and in brewing their drinks.

People were happy on that shore. There was plenty to eat. It was never too hot, never too cold, never too wet, never too dry. Men talked with the beasts and were at peace with one another.

Then there came an afternoon when Maco went to take the fish out of his trap on the edge of the ocean. To his surprise, someone had been there before him. His net was torn. The fish were all gone from it. He could not understand anything like this. But he mended his net and set the trap up once again.

Next day, and the next day, the same thing took place.

"I shall have to set someone here to watch my trap," Maco said to himself. And while the youth was mending his net, a woodpecker lit on a tree branch over his head.

"Woodpecker," said Maco, "will you guard my trap for me? Peck on the tree trunk when anyone touches it."

The very next morning Maco thought he heard the sharp tap-tap-tap of the bird's beak against the tree trunk. But a woodpecker's tapping is not very loud, so he waited to be sure. Then he heard it again—tap-tap-tap. The young man ran as fast as ever he could. But he was too late. The trap was broken and the robber was gone.

"I must find someone who can make a louder noise," Maco thought. So he called on the cuckoo. "Friend, will you guard my trap? Give a loud 'cuck-oo' as soon as anyone touches it."

It was not long before the call of the cuckoo rang through the air. *"Kuk-kuk! Kuk-kuk!"*

Maco ran swiftly, and he reached the trap in time to see a young man with a crocodile's head tearing the net to shreds with his sharp teeth. Angry, Maco raised his bow. He sent an arrow straight between the eyes of the robber. With a cry, the crocodile-man rolled over dead and slid down the bank into the ocean.

The next day, the cuckoo's loud call came again. *"Kuk-kuk! Kuk-kuk! Kuk-kuk!"* Maco ran to see whether another crocodile-man was there. But instead he found a young girl. Tears rolled down her cheeks, and yet, in spite of them, she was beautiful.

"Who are you, girl? What are you doing here? Where is your home?" Maco spoke gently so as not to frighten the lovely stranger.

But the girl only wept harder. She held out a leather sandal and said, "This belongs to my brother, and I fear ill fate has come to him. He went to find food for us, and now he is gone."

Maco recognized the sandal for it had fallen from the foot of the crocodile-man. But he said nothing. He did not want to tell the girl that he was the cause of her sorrow.

In reply to his other questions, the stranger told him that her name was Ana. She and her brother had been out on the ocean in their dugout canoe when a storm blew them far from home. Their boat had been lost, and they had had to swim to this shore. She was all alone now, and she did not know what to do.

The young man led the weeping girl home to his mother. The old woman comforted her and gave her shelter. Ana lived in Maco's hut for many days, and it is not at all strange that the two handsome young people fell in love with one another.

At last, Maco found courage to tell Ana how her brother had met his death. He explained that it had happened while the crocodile-man was destroying his fish trap. This, the girl knew, had given him the right to use his bow and arrow. And she loved him so much that she did not say no when he asked her to be his wife.

21

"But I cannot marry you, Maco, without my father's consent," she said. This was the rule in those times in that land. "My father will never permit us to wed. He does not like handsome men. He surely will kill you in revenge if he finds out that you killed his son."

"Then let us be married first," Maco said. "We can ask his consent later. He need never know just how your brother came to his death."

So they were married, and Maco began to make his canoe ready for the long journey.

But Ana was troubled. "Let me go first, my dear husband," she begged. "My father has truly a terrible temper. He may well do you harm if you do not please him."

Maco, however, would not hear of his young wife's taking his canoe alone out on the sea. So they set forth together.

When they came near Ana's home village, her young husband persuaded her that he should go on ahead. Maco wanted first to secure the blessing of her parents so that her homecoming would be happy.

"Take care! Take care!" his wife said. "My mother will offer you first a clay bowl filled with raw meat. Then she will hold out a second bowl filled with manioc cakes. Take care how you choose!"

It happened just so. The woman greeted her son-in-law with the two bowls. When Maco chose the manioc cakes, he could see she was pleased. She had made them herself that very day.

"You choose well, my son. I give you my blessing," the girl's mother smiled. "But it will not be so easy with Ana's father. He does not like men with handsome faces like yours. And he is terrible in anger. We must go softly. Ana and I had better see him first."

But even the two women, his own wife and daughter, could not calm the man's anger when he met the young man. Maco thought it was strange that his wife's father should be wearing a great hollow gourd, a huge calabash, over his head. But of course, he said nothing.

Maco could not see the man's face, but he could hear the rough words that came out from under the calabash hood.

"How dared you marry my daughter without my consent?" the man under the calabash fairly screamed.

"I'm sorry, Tata." Maco gave him the affectionate name he would have given his own father. "It was not right that Ana and I should marry without her parents' consent. But if you will only give us your blessing now, I will do whatever you say. I will work for you. I will make for you everything that you may ask for."

"Then make me a stool," Ana's father roared. "Carve it of wood. And let its base be exactly like my own head. It must look just like me, or you shall be killed."

"How can I carve your head in the wood, Tata? I never have seen it, for you hide it under a calabash."

"That is your affair, young man." This was the only answer that came from under the hollow gourd.

When Maco begged his wife to tell him what her father's face was like, she shook her head.

"My father sees all, and my father knows all. He surely would find out that I had told you. Then he would kill us both."

All Maco could do was to hide in the bushes beside the man's hammock and hope that, while he slept, the calabash would fall

24

off and his face might be seen.

In those times, as has been said, all living creatures helped one another. It was the insects who came to the aid of this good young man. A flea bit the hand of the sleeping man. But he only grunted and turned on his other side. A spider nipped the man's neck. He merely brushed it away.

But now there came a whole army of little black ants. They crawled under his calabash, and they tormented him so that he had to lift it off to get rid of them.

Maco thus had a good look at his father-in-law's face. Like his son, this man had the head of a crocodile. The young man remembered the story of how it was in the beginning of the world. How some of the sons of the very first crocodile had heads like that beast!

Well, now, he could carve the wooden stool. It was quite ready when morning came. And its base was just as Ana's father had ordered that it should be.

What could the Man-with-the-Crocodile-Head do now but bless the marriage of his daughter, Ana, and this remarkable youth?

But even when he had been taken in as a member of Ana's tribe, Maco did not feel happy. He knew well that his wife's father was jealous of his good looks. But even more, he was worried about his own dear mother. Was she in good health? Did she have need of him? He felt that he must find out for himself.

Her father refused to let Ana go away again. So with a sad heart, Maco set out alone. He promised he would come back just as soon as he could.

His mother welcomed him with great joy, for in truth all was well with her. His neighbors begged the young man not to go back to his wife's tribe. Even the Wise Man of the village warned Maco that great trouble awaited him there.

Maco did not heed the warning, however. He had given his promise, and he must go back to the Crocodile's daughter. And trouble did come.

Somehow the secret of his son's death had come to the ears of the Crocodile-Man. So when Maco arrived his furious father-in-law was waiting with his bow and arrow ready. His aim was good. His arrow sped to the heart of the poor young husband.

The Crocodile dragged Maco's body to the edge of a cliff that hung over the ocean. He threw it far out and down into the water below. And he said, "You ended my son's life. Now I've ended yours."

With that ugly deed, trouble came into the world. Men ceased to live in peace with one another. Winds blew so hard that big trees and small huts were often thrown to the ground. Lightning flashed. Thunder roared. The rain fell in torrents. And the rivers flowed out of their beds and over the land.

The jaguar ate up the little agouty. Snakes' fangs now held poison. Oh, the world was a different place.

Poor Ana could not be comforted. She ran along the seashore looking for her lost husband. At last, when she reached the cliff, she spied Maco there in the deep water below. So she too jumped off. Far, far down in the ocean, she joined her beloved.

They say that even today no one speaks loudly on the edge of that cliff. No one wants to disturb the Crocodile's daughter and her young lover who live happily together there in their watery home.

THE YOUTH WHO MADE FRIENDS WITH
THE BEASTS AND THE BIRDS

THE FORESTS of South America's warm northern lands are filled with animals of many kinds and birds of many hues. There are foxes and jaguars. There are parrots with feathers of green, red and yellow, blue, orange and gray. Men gather these feathers for making robes and headdresses for their festival dances. And in this tale, there is a house with a feather roof.

What a sight that must have been! Red feathers and yellow feathers! They were laid one over the other so close that the rain could not get through, just as it is when they are on a bird's back. One would think that many moons must have come and gone before enough feathers for such a roof could be gathered. But as this story tells it, they were found all in one day.

It happened this way.

In that part of the land there was a rich man. Oh, indeed he was rich. He owned so many llamas that he had never counted them all.

But if he was the richest, the poor young hero in the story must have been the poorest. He lived all alone in a tiny hut on the mountainside, and often there was nothing to eat in his cooking pot. This youth had no mother, and his father was a hermit who was said to dwell inside a great egg on the top of the mountain peak.

The poor youth's name was Huathiacuri, which is pronounced Wâ·tyâ·kū′rē. His father was Paricaca, who was known to be wise. Some people thought Paricaca was a god. The story does not say so, but it clearly shows that this Man-Who-Lived-in-an-Egg was far more clever than most other men. That is why whenever Huathiacuri was in trouble, he climbed the mountain to ask advice from his father.

Again and again Paricaca said to his son, "Be kind to the beasts! Be kind to the birds! I will teach you how to talk with them so that you can understand what they say. Do them a good turn whenever you can. Then they will come to your aid when you need a friend."

This bit of advice, Paricaca said, was more important than anything else he could teach Huathiacuri.

The youth obeyed his wise father. He made friends with all the beasts and the birds he met in the forest trails. He understood the birdcalls. He could talk with serpents and foxes. And he had no fear of any, not even of jaguars.

One day this young man came to a fine house. Indeed, it was finer than any house he ever had seen. And from the men working in its garden, he learned about the rich man who owned it.

"Our master is great. No other in this land is so rich as he. And he is proud. Sometimes he boasts that the gods are no more important. Yet inside this house he lies ill, and he cannot make himself well again."

As they spoke, there came through the door the beautiful daughter of the very rich man. Her name in the story was Tanca, and so Tanca she should be called. Huathiacuri thought he never had seen so fair a creature. So great was the love he suddenly felt for her that he forgot his poor clothes and dared to speak.

"Good day, señorita," he bowed low. "I wish you good day."

"Alas, stranger," the girl replied, "no day can be good until my dear father is well again. This doctor and that doctor have been called to his bedside. But none of them has cured him."

"If I can find a cure, señorita, will you be my bride?"

What could he have been thinking? She was so rich! So beautiful! And he was so poor! He must have been quite out of his wits with love for the girl, Tanca.

"I shall find a cure for your father. Yes, I can find the reason why he lies so ill. But in return you must marry me." Huathiacuri was thinking that his father, the wise Man-Who-Lived-in-an-Egg on the mountain top, would surely know what to do.

The rich man's daughter looked at the eager young stranger. It was true that he did not make such a fine figure as other suitors who had wanted her for their wife. His clothes were poor. But his face was kind. And she did not say, "no."

"I cannot hope you will succeed where so many doctors have failed," Tanca replied. "But I'll tell my father. You shall see him yourself when you come back with his cure."

Huathiacuri climbed the mountain to consult his wise father. But to his great dismay, all Paricaca would say was, "Remember what I have told you, my son! Be kind to the beasts! Be kind to the birds! Help them, and they will help you in your time of need."

The young man's heart sank. He did not see how the animals or the birds could make the sick man well. But all the same, on his journey back, he went out of his way to let two young foxes out of a trap. And it was from these grateful animals that he

learned the secret of the cure he was seeking.

"The rich man is bewitched, Huathiacuri," they said. "Tanca's stepmother, his second wife, is the cause of his illness. She has been cheating him for a stranger, who visits her in the form of a serpent. She has been giving him corn and other treasures that belong to her husband.

"Find the serpent in the rich man's storehouse! Look, also, for the serpent's servant, the two-headed toad that sits beside the big millstone! When these two have been killed, the man will get well."

Huathiacuri rejoiced. He ran as fast as he could back to the rich man's house.

"I have the cure for your father's illness," he told Tanca. "But only if you will marry me, will I make him well."

Tanca did not say "yes," but she did not say "no." Her father gave his consent to the bargain, however. He knew that he would soon die if help did not come to him quickly.

Then, before all the members of that household, the young man said to the rich man, "You are under an evil spell, good sir. And it is your wife who is the cause of it. She has been giving your corn and your other treasures to a stranger who comes secretly here in the form of a serpent. It is he who has bewitched you. It is he who makes you ill so that you may not see she is cheating you.

"Kill that serpent which crawls into your storehouse! Kill also his servant, the two-headed toad by the millstone! Then you will be well."

Tanca's stepmother declared that Huathiacuri was lying. But when the serpent and the toad had been killed, and her husband rose from his bed, well and strong, she wept. She said she, too, had been bewitched and forced to give the snake-man their treasures. But no one believed her.

For Huathiacuri, Tanca's father had nothing but gratitude and high praise. And he ordered a great feast to celebrate the wedding of his daughter and the young man who had saved his life.

It was then that the girl's stepbrother objected.

"My sister shall never marry this stranger. Who is he? He looks to be a weak fellow. Let him match me in a contest of drinking and dancing! That will prove if he is worthy."

Now Huathiacuri did not want to cause trouble, so he agreed. But first he ran up the mountainside to seek the advice of Paricaca, his father. This time as before the wise Man-Who-Lived-in-an-Egg said only, "The most important thing to remember is to be kind to the beasts and the birds. Then they will come to your aid."

As the young man ran down the mountain again, he saw the same two little foxes, off in the bushes. "They helped me before," he said to himself, "perhaps they will help me again." Being a good hunter, he killed two plump rabbits. And he laid them down on the path for the foxes to eat.

When they finished their meal, Huathiacuri told them of the contests that awaited him at his bride's home. The foxes disappeared into the bushes. And when they came out again, one carried a gourd filled with a magic drink. The other had a flute with one hundred pipes. They told their friend, Huathiacuri, just what he must do.

Then, with his magic gourd and his flute, he ran as fast as he could to try his luck against Tanca's stepbrother.

Chicha was the name of the drink in the foxes' gourd. The youth drank one bowlful of chicha after another. Somehow that gourd never was empty. He drank and he drank, with no trouble at all. Everyone said he had won the drinking contest.

On the foxes' flute with its one hundred pipes, Huathiacuri played such sweet music, and he danced so well, that he won that match also. But the girl's stepbrother was still not satisfied.

"Whoever heard of a bridegroom in such shabby clothes?" he asked. "Let the fellow show us how he will appear at the feast. We can then decide whether his costume is as good as mine."

This time Paricaca himself came to the aid of his son. He told Huathiacuri where to find the skin of a jaguar which some hunters had killed. With this thrown over his shoulders, the bridegroom stood proudly before the wedding guests. A brilliant rainbow played over the black spots and the circles on the tawny fur mantle. Everyone gasped in wonder. Never had so fine a sight been seen in the land. The surly stepbrother had been bested again. But still he complained.

"No home has this stranger to offer a wife," he said. "Let him build her a house. I will build a house, too. He who builds most quickly and best shall decide when the wedding shall take place. And I shall say, 'Never!'"

Well, they began to build. Tanca's stepbrother had all his father's servants to help him. Huathiacuri had only his own two hands. So, of course, the brother's house rose more quickly into the air. It was ready for its roof while the poor youth was still at work on his walls.

"Now, truly I am in trouble," he said to himself. But he remembered his father's words "Be kind to the beasts and the birds, and they will help you when you need them."

He appealed to all his four-footed and feathered friends. And

33

at once they came running and flying out of the forest. The jaguar and the fox, the deer and the tapir, even snakes and armadillos found ways in which they could help. They worked all through the night, and when morning came, the youth's house, also, was ready for its roof.

Now, the son of the rich man had his father's llamas to carry the straw thatch for his roof. One after another, the small sturdy beasts marched along with great bundles of straw on their backs.

But Huathiacuri's friends, the jaguars, attacked them. At the very first roars of these fierce wildcats, the timid llamas were frightened. They ran away, scattering the straw to the four winds.

It was then that the sky was darkened by the wings of thousands of birds. There were wee hummingbirds, white bellbirds, green parrots, red birds, and bluebirds. Each one had a feather held tight in its beak. The red feathers and the yellow feathers were laid in a pattern upon the roof. Those of other colors made a bright rainbow border. And so closely were they all fitted together that the feather roof would shed water far better than a roof made of thatch.

"Now Brother-of-My-Bride, let us get along with the wedding!" Huathiacuri was losing his patience. So, too, were the guests.

"The wedding! The wedding!" they cried.

And Tanca added her voice. "I will marry this clever young man this very day." But the ill-natured stepbrother still scowled. He had thought of one more way to test Huathiacuri. It would be a footrace between the two of them.

"Agreed!" said Huathiacuri. "I will race. But beware! If I pass you, bad luck will come to you."

The race was run. Over the plains and into the forest, the two

34

young men ran like the wind. The brother was a little ahead of Huathiarcuri when suddenly the jaguars roared. The foxes barked. All the beasts made horrid noises. The din was so terrifying that Tanca's stepbrother was frightened. He slowed his pace for a moment and Huathiacuri ran past him, touching him on the shoulder.

Perhaps it was by the magic of Paricaca or some other spirit— for at this touch the stepbrother was turned into a deer, which disappeared into the forest and was not seen again.

At last Tanca and Huathiacuri could have their wedding feast in peace, and they lived happily in their house with its fine feather roof. The bride's father was so grateful to her young husband that he gave them a goodly share of his riches for he had enough for all.

JABUTY, THE STRONG

COULD THE ANIMALS truly talk, long, long ago?

Could men understand them?

Who knows for sure?

They certainly talk among themselves. A hen talks to her chickens. A cow talks to her calf. It may be that a frisky horse understands the barking of the playful dog that snaps at his heels.

Men could have been wiser in those ancient times. They must have been able to speak with the beasts and the birds. How else would there be so many old tales about the animals and their doings?

If one believes these old tales, the animals did talk. And just as men can, they could think up clever ways in which to get the best of one another. Take the story of *Jabuty, the Strong*, which tells how this little land tortoise outwitted a whale and a tapir.

Perhaps it was not actually a whale. It might have been only a porpoise or a manatee, a strange water creature that weighs more than four hundred pounds. That would have been big enough to be taken for a small whale.

One day a brown land tortoise of the kind which in South Amer-

36

ica is called a *jabuty*, crawled down to the seashore to take a dip. Just as he reached the edge of the water, a young whale poked his nose above the incoming waves.

"Hello, Jabuty, what are you doing here?" the whale asked. "I thought you lived on the land."

"I do live on the land. But also I like to cool my shell in the ocean when the day is hot."

"Well, well, Little Short Legs, you must be tired after such a long walk. Such a poor, weak creature you are. And you carry such a big shell. No wonder you are hot. You'd best squat down and rest before you try to swim."

In this manner, the young whale made fun of the tortoise. He teased him and teased him, until at last the jabuty grew angry. He was so angry, indeed, that he scarcely thought what he was saying when he replied. "My legs may be short, O Whale, but I am not weak. In my part of the land I am called Jabuty, the Strong. And strong I am, just as strong as you are."

"Ho! Ho! Ho! Ho! Short Legs is as strong as a whale! Ho-o-o-o!" The whale laughed and laughed. He rolled over and over in the blue ocean. He blew a white jet of water high into the air.

When the jabuty saw the size of this giant fish, it may well be he was sorry he had made such a wild boast. But if he were, he gave no sign. Instead, foolish creature, he only boasted the more.

"Yes, Whale, I am called Jabuty, the Strong. I will wager I am even stronger than you. I could prove this if only I had a vine long enough to tie around your tail. With such a line, I could pull you right out of the ocean and up onto this shore."

Then the whale laughed even louder. He blew a second jet of water higher into the air. But he was annoyed that such a small creature as this land tortoise should dare to stand up to him.

"Ho! Just let me see you try to pull me ashore!" the whale cried. "A long, strong vine is easy to find in the forest. Why don't you go get one, Little Short Legs? Or are you afraid?"

"Well, then, I will," the jabuty said. Perhaps he had already thought of a plan to get himself out of this tight place. Or perhaps the plan came to him when he met a huge tapir, crashing through a thicket of bushes and vines.

Now the tapir is a curious four-legged animal which grows as big as a small cow. It has a tough bristly hide and muscles like iron. Indeed, a tapir is one of the strongest of the animals that live on the land, just as the whale is the strongest fish that swims in the sea.

The tapir's pointed snout is longer than that of any other animal's but the elephant. Its thick body is round like that of a giant hog. It must have frightened the jabuty just to see this beast coming towards him.

"Good day, Jabuty! What are you looking for?" the tapir asked gruffly.

"Good day, friend Tapir, I've come to this thicket to find me a long, strong vine."

"Whatever will you do with such a vine, Short Legs?"

"I'll tie it around your neck and drag you down to the ocean," the silly tortoise replied. Or perhaps he was not so silly. It may have been at that moment that his good idea came to him.

"Ho! Ho! Ho!" the tapir laughed just as loud as the whale had.

"You may laugh, Tapir, but it is not for nothing that I am known as Jabuty, the Strong. Let me knot this round your neck," he said, pulling a long, long vine off a tall tree.

"I'll take its other end and go down to the seashore. When I

38

shake the vine, you must move quickly towards the forest. We shall then see which of us is the stronger, for indeed I shall pull you into the sea. When you are tired, give the vine two hard shakes as a sign you want to rest."

"This is a good game," the tapir thought. And he said to the tortoise, "Have it your own way. But take care, Jabuty! Take care that you do pull me into the sea! If instead I should drag you back into this thicket, I'll stamp on your brown shell and break it into small bits."

The jabuty took the other end of the vine into his mouth. He crawled down to the seashore where the young whale was waiting. The big fish was still laughing at the idea of their tug-of-war.

When the jabuty had tied the vine securely about the tail of the whale, he said, "Now wait until I have gone back into the forest. When I am ready I will shake the vine. Then you must swim away, into the ocean. Swim as hard as you can. Dive as deep as you like. Still I will pull you back to the shore. Should you grow tired and wish to rest, shake the vine three times."

The little jabuty crawled into the thicket. When he was well out of sight of both the whale and the tapir, he shook the vine. Then he peeped from his hiding place under a bush to see what would happen.

The whale dived into the waves. He dived deep. And so strong was his swimming that he dragged the huge tapir, on the other end of the vine, through the forest. On and on, the tapir felt himself sliding over the ground.

"How can this be?" the puzzled tapir was shocked. "This jabuty is truly strong. I had no notion he would move me at all."

The tapir struggled with all his might. Somehow or other he got

39

a foothold in the earth. Little by little, by pulling and tugging, he inched his way back into the forest again.

Then it was the turn of the young whale to be surprised. When he found himself being dragged towards the shore, he said to himself, "Well, well, Little Short Legs is correctly named Jabuty, the Strong. I shall have to work harder."

With his great tail thrashing the waves, the whale pulled on the jabuty's long, strong vine. Again the tapir lost ground. When the whale dived, he was pulled far towards the water. He was so busy that he had no time to think about the jabuty. If he had, no doubt he would have supposed that the tortoise had buried himself in the sand.

The strange tug-of-war went on and on, while the cunning jabuty watched from under his bush. First the tapir was ahead. Then the whale. Now the whale seemed to be getting the best of the contest. Then it was the tapir. At last both of them grew tired of the whole business. Both shook the vine as a sign they wanted to rest.

The jabuty was gleeful.

"It is now the right moment to end the game," he said to himself. And he cut the vine at its middle. The end of the half nearest the tapir, he tied around a tree. He took up the other end in his mouth, and he crawled down to the seashore. There the young whale was resting, afloat on top of the waves.

"Are you satisfied now, Whale? Was I not right? Am I not stronger than you? Or shall we begin again our tug-of-war?" The land tortoise was cocky.

The whale looked at the jabuty. He could not understand how the little creature could be so fresh and so gay.

"You were right, O Jabuty, the Strong. I am content, I give you the victory. Truly you have better muscles than I."

Now the jabuty wet his back well. One would think he had just come out of the sea. Untying the rest of the vine from around the tree trunk, he took its other end in his mouth and went in search of the tapir. Like the whale, this big beast had used up all his strength. He lay, breathing hard, on the floor of the forest.

"Ho, mighty Tapir, why did you not pull me back into the thicket with you? Was I not right? Am I not well named Jabuty, the Strong?"

"You were right, Jabuty. You truly are strong." The tapir's voice sounded as if he hardly believed the words he spoke. How, indeed, could it be that this weak, slow-moving creature was so perky after such a mighty struggle?

The jabuty untied the vine from around the tapir's neck. And the big beast went wearily off into the forest. There was now nothing said about his breaking the turtle's brown shell to bits. And neither the tapir nor the whale ever called the jabuty Little Short Legs again.

THE JABUTY AND THE JAGUAR

THERE IS A Brazilian riddle that goes like this: A house on four low posts, with a roof of hard shell. What is it?

And the answer, of course, is a tortoise, a jabuty like the one in the story of the whale and the tapir.

That was a good tale, but some people think that the name Jabuty, the Strong was not right for that tortoise. Instead, they say, he should have been called Jabuty, the Clever One.

Strong he was not, but cunning and clever he was. Cunning he had to be, for there were, all around him, animals bigger than he —who wanted to eat him.

It is better, far better, for man or beast to be quick-witted rather than to be just strong and swift. The jaguar ran faster; yet the jabuty won the race. The jaguar was stronger; but usually the jabuty got the best of him. Here is a story that proves this point.

There was a day in a Brazilian rain forest, when a jabuty was crawling along under the trees. A monkey on a branch over his head, wanting to tease him, threw a hard nut down upon his round shell.

"Hurry along there, Jabuty, before I throw down another nut

and break your back. Run as fast as you can on your little short legs." Like the other jungle animals he enjoyed poking fun at the poor slow-moving tortoise.

"It is true, I go slowly now, Monkey," the Jabuty said mildly. "But it was not always like this. Once I had hard hoofs instead of these soft claw feet.

"One day I was sitting by a path, cleaning my hoofs, and a deer came along. At that time the deer could not run so swiftly as he does today. For it was he who wore soft claw feet, and I who wore hoofs.

"That deer spoke to me politely, saying, 'Good day, Friend Jabuty, those are good shoes you have. Be so very good as to let me try them on.'

"I was pleased with his praise of my strong, horny hoofs. Silly fool that I was, I let him put them on his own feet. Of course, he found out that they helped him to run swiftly. He dashed off into the forest, and he never came back. What was there for me to do but to use his claw feet? And that is one of the reasons why I crawl so slowly now."

"Poor Little Short Legs! That was too bad." The monkey felt sorry for the good-natured tortoise. He thought to do him a kindness when he gave him this warning. "Take care, Friend Jabuty! Keep your eyes open! The jaguar hunts today."

Not very much farther along the path, the jabuty came face to face with the jaguar. "Here's a tender mouthful for me." The big wildcat licked his lips. "Turtle meat is good eating. But how is it that this little fellow does not seem afraid of me. Perhaps he is stronger than I think. Perhaps I'd better talk with him a while first, before I try to kill him."

44

Under his brown shell, the poor jabuty was really quaking with fear and thinking, I am in trouble here. I shall need all my wits to get out of this alive. But he made no sign.

"I am the king of this jungle," the jaguar roared. "I am mighty, and I like fresh meat." But still the jabuty showed none of his fear.

"You may be king of this jungle, O Jaguar, but I, too, am strong. I, too, eat meat. I can eat even more fresh meat than you can."

The tortoise, no doubt, thought to make up for his small size and his weakness with these bold boasting words.

"Ho! Ho! Jabuty, I do not believe that. But we can see. I killed a deer this morning. You shall have a chunk of its meat. I'll take another chunk, just the same size. We shall begin our meal at the same time. Then we can prove which of us can eat the most."

"Agreed," said the jabuty. "But you must give me your promise that we shall eat with closed eyes. I can chew better that way."

At the word "Go!" the two animals shut their eyes tight. They began to gnaw at the two large chunks of deer meat.

The great jaguar gobbled with enormous bites of his sharp teeth. And the little jabuty nibbled away as fast as he could with his tiny jaws.

Every now and again, the tortoise opened his narrow eyes a wee bit. His heart grew heavy when he saw how much the jaguar was eating. So little seemed to be gone from his own chunk of the deer meat.

At last, through the narrow slits between his wrinkled eyelids, he noticed that the jaguar was eating more slowly. The big cat's stomach was bulging. Soon he could eat no more.

The jaguar lay with closed eyes, resting before he would make a last try. It was a hot day, and he fell fast asleep.

Quickly the cunning tortoise dragged the small piece of meat in front of the jaguar over to his own place. Softly, softly, he tugged at his uneaten chunk until it lay between the paws of his enemy. This done, he called out "Halloo, there, Friend Jaguar! I can eat no more. My stomach is full. Let us open our eyes and see which of us has won this eating match."

The jaguar blinked his eyes. He wondered at the wee bit of meat that lay in front of the jabuty, and at the great chunk that lay between his own paws.

"I must say, Jabuty, you can eat more than I can. You must indeed be strong if you eat so much meat. But you can never be so quick as I am. I could beat you in a race. Of that I am sure." He was ashamed that he had been bested by such a small creature.

"Let us race to the river and back here again. Then we shall see which of us travels fastest," he said.

"Now, indeed, here is trouble!" the jabuty thought. "I must make a plan." But he did not show he was afraid.

"Done! I'll race you gladly," he said. "But not today. It is far to the river, and we have just eaten. When the dawn comes again, the race shall take place." He needed time.

Well, the jaguar had just had a good meal. He was no longer hungry, so he was willing to wait for his taste of fresh turtle meat. He lay down to nap again, well pleased and quite sure the race would be his.

But the jabuty did not sleep. Not that afternoon, nor all through the night. Instead he called on his brothers, his cousins, and his uncles. And he bribed them to hide themselves every few yards along the route of the race.

When the birds sang in the dawn, the jabuty and the jaguar set

46

out from their starting place to run to the river and back. With a mighty bound, the swift wildcat crashed through the jungle, leaving the tortoise far, far behind.

When he had gone about halfway to the river, he called out "Jabuty, Jabuty, halloo, Jabuty, Jabuty, where are you?"

To his surprise, the answering call came from ahead of him, not from behind.

"Halloo, Halloo! Here Jaguar!" With his own eyes, the cat spied the brown shell of a tortoise moving along in the bushes. So he bounded more swiftly on through the jungle.

"Halloo!" he called when the river was in sight. "Halloo!" came the answer from the stream. In the distance he saw a tortoise crawling under a bush.

Faster and faster he ran. But always he found a tortoise ahead of him. When at last he came, panting, back to the starting point, the jabuty was there, patiently waiting.

"Friend Jabuty, you are strong indeed, and quick as well." The jaguar shook his head, wondering. "But I am more skillful than you, that I know. Let us try one more contest! Let us see which one of us is the best hand at painting. Your shell is plain brown. My coat is plain tan. Both of us would look better if our coats had designs upon them. You shall paint my back. I shall paint your shell. But woe be to you, Jabuty, if you do not make me the most splendid of all the beasts of the jungle!"

"This is the worst trouble of all," said the tortoise, shaking inside his shell. "I need all my wits now, if I am to come out of this alive."

Well, the jabuty and the jaguar took turns dipping their paint brushes in the colors they chose. What kind of paints could these be? The tale does not say. But anyone who has ever seen a jabuty

and a jaguar can guess who won that contest. For the rough markings on the round shell of the tortoise are muddy and uneven. On the other hand the jaguar has neat black spots and rosettes upon its tawny body and legs, its head and its tail.

"I must say, you have won again," the jaguar said to the jabuty. He did not sound angry. He was too pleased with the handsome spotted coat which the tortoise had given him. "You are strong. You are swift. You are clever at painting. But still, it is I who am king of the jungle. I am hungry now. Now I shall eat you for my supper."

"Of all my great troubles with the jaguar, here is the greatest. How shall I escape his hungry jaws?" The tortoise thought quickly. Then he said to the jaguar, "What must be, must be, O, King of the Jungle! But before you eat me and lie down to your rest, take one more look at yourself in the river. See how handsome you are now. I have made you the most splendid of all animals. Come, look at yourself, Jaguar, here in the clear water."

The vain jaguar stood on the edge of the river's pool and gazed at his reflection. He purred with delight at the neat rosettes and spots on his tawny coat.

So intent was he upon the fine sight he saw in the pool that he failed to notice the jabuty crawling noiselessly towards a long hollow log. He turned only in time to see the little hind legs and the tiny tail of the tortoise disappearing into this safe shelter.

He was cross, and he roared fiercely as he lay down with his yellow cat eyes fixed on the open end of the log. For all anyone knows, the jaguar is still there, waiting for the jabuty to come out again. It is more likely, however, that the quick-witted tortoise crawled out of the other end of the log and got safely away.

A TRICK THAT FAILED

CONIRAYA WAS THE NAME people of the Southern Andes gave to a forest spirit who liked to play tricks. A curious spirit he was, and powerful too. He could change himself into any form that he chose.

Sometimes he pretended to be the High God, the Maker-of-All-Things himself. At other times he appeared dressed like a poor Indian whose only poncho was the sun. Then his clothes were in rags. His face was smeared with dirt. It was no wonder that people thought he was a filthy beggar to be kicked out of the way.

One day, this Coniraya decided it was time for him to take a wife. As he walked through the villages in his ragged disguise, he saw a young girl whose name was Cavillaca. She was the prettiest in all that neighborhood, and everyone loved her. So, of course, it was she whom Coniraya decided to have for his wife.

One afternoon, Cavillaca sat with her weaving loom at the foot of a tall tree. Her fingers moved carefully as she wove. She did not lift her eyes from her work. And so she did not notice Coniraya who had taken on the form of a bird. So intent was she on her weaving that she did not hear him when he lit on a branch just over her head.

50

In his beak, the forest spirit carried a tiny seed. It was one of the precious seeds from which men were born, so people said, then Coniraya hid the seed inside one of the ripe fruits which grew on the tree. With his sharp beak, he pecked at the stem of the fruit until it fell into the lap of the girl weaving below.

Cavillaca stopped her work just long enough to eat the delicious fruit. Of course, as she did so, she swallowed the precious seed which Coniraya had put into it. And in time there was born to her a fine baby boy.

Who can have given Cavillaca the seed of life? the girl's neighbors wondered. They asked the name of her husband, and they did not believe her when she said she did not know. But, in truth, Cavillaca was quite as puzzled as the village folk. And when her baby grew older, she often was sad.

"A child needs a father," she thought. "Who is the man who gave me the seed of my son's life? How shall I find out?"

"There is a way, *niña*," said the Wise Woman to whom the girl went for advice. "Gather the young men of the village together. Place the child among them. Then pray to the gods to guide him to his father."

So it was arranged. All the young men of that village came to its open square. Each was dressed in his best, for each wanted, above all things, to wed fair Cavillaca.

Not only the young men of that village were there. Youths from neighboring villages came too, rich ones and poor ones. There was even a beggar clad in filthy rags. This one was the forest spirit, Coniraya, the Trickster, in his favorite disguise.

Cavillaca gave one look at him, standing there so shabby and so dirty. Then she turned quickly away, saying to herself, "Surely

51

the gods did not give me such a man for a husband."

The young mother set her child down in the center of the circle of young men. Then she lifted her arms to the sky and prayed aloud. "Oh, Mighty Spirits, show us the truth. Lead my child to his father that I may claim him for my husband."

The small boy stood for a moment inside the circle of eager young men. Then, turning to neither right nor left, he toddled straight to the beggar and held out his chubby arms.

Cavillaca gave a cry. "I will not have that filthy man for my husband. I will not! I will not!"

She caught her child up into her arms, and she fled from the square.

By means of his magic, Coniraya then threw off his soiled beggar's rags. He appeared before the people, dressed like a god, in garments that shone bright as the sun. Adorned with fine golden ornaments he made a fine sight. Everyone was amazed.

"Come back, Cavillaca! Come back!" They shouted to the girl to return and see the miracle which had taken place. But she would not turn around. With the horrid picture of the beggar's dirty face fixed in her mind, she ran and she ran, until she disappeared in the forest.

Somehow the girl was able to run faster than the spirit. She sped through the trees and down to the very edge of the sea. Not looking ahead of her, she plunged into the water with her child still in her arms. No doubt it was the High God himself who saved them from drowning by turning them to stone. A tall thin rock, and a smaller rock, they stood there in the sea with their heads out of the water.

Coniraya was angry that his trick had turned out so badly. He went here. He went there. Everywhere he searched for his lost bride and his son.

At one place, upon a high cliff, he met a huge bird, a condor.

"Have you seen Cavillaca," he asked. "Did the girl and her baby run this way?" And the bird replied. "Oh, yes, Friend, I saw her with her child in her arms. She must be quite near."

The condor's words brought hope and comfort to Coniraya, and he was pleased.

"For your good news, my brother, you shall be blessed," he said. "Let it be known the world over that the man who kills a condor brings bad luck to himself."

So it has always been. Bold is the hunter who dares to shoot one of these redheaded black giants of the bird world.

Well, Coniraya went on with his search. And soon he met a red fox.

"Have you seen Cavillaca?" he asked eagerly. "Did a pretty girl with a little boy in her arms come running this way?"

"No," the fox replied curtly. "No such ones have I seen. Go where you will, you won't find them again."

The forest spirit was angry. He feared that the cruel fox had spoken the truth. And like everyone else he did not like to hear bad news.

"For your evil words, O Fox, you shall be cursed," he cried. "A strong, unpleasant odor shall cling to your fur. Your scent shall ride on the air, and by it hunters shall find you. Only at night shall it be safe for you to come out of your den."

And that is how it still is. Hunting dogs can smell a fox when it is yet some distance away. Only in the dark do wise foxes roam over the land.

54

While Coniraya was traveling through the woods and the plains looking for his lost bride, he met a huge jaguar. To this fierce beast he also put his questions. "Have you seen Cavillaca? Did she come this way?"

The jaguar roared, "Yes Friend, the girl is not far away. You surely will find her in time. Do not give up hope."

"Brother, I thank you. Your words are welcome." Coniraya was pleased. "Blessings be upon you!" he cried. "You shall be the most powerful of all the beasts in this land. In life, men shall admire you and fear you. In death, they shall honor you. The bravest of the young hunters shall bear your head proudly in their dances. With your keen eyes still blazing, with your long teeth showing fiercely, you shall still seem alive."

And in that part of the land when there was a festival, the dancers indeed wore a jaguar skin thrown over their shoulders, with the head as a crown.

But the jaguar's words did not come true. Coniraya searched, and he asked help from every creature he met. When he came upon a bright red and green parrot, he was discouraged.

"Brother Parrot," he begged, "Give me some hope. You fly low. You fly high. Surely you must have seen the girl, Cavillaca, with her little boy in her arms?"

Now the parrot showed even less sympathy than the fox had.

"No such girl have I seen and no little boy. You may as well give up your search, for you never will find her."

When Coniraya heard the parrot's cruel prediction, he was even more angry than he had been with the fox.

"Harsh words come out of your mouth, Parrot," he cried. "And harsh shall your voice ever be. Your cries shall ring through this forest as loud and as unpleasant as your words sound in my ears. Your slightest whisper shall come out through your beak shrill and sharp, so that your enemies may hear you from afar."

That, so these people of the Southern Andes mountains say, is why the voice of the parrot splits one's ears. He squawks and he screams even when he is not angry. And no one could enjoy his song even if he tried to sing sweetly.

Did Coniraya ever find his lost bride? Some say he did. At last he reached the place on the shore where she had rushed into the sea. There a jabuty pointed out the two rocks which rose out of the waves.

"There is your lost bride with her son by her side. I saw them enter the sea. And straightaway they turned to rocks. Silly Coniraya, that was a poor trick you played on the bride who would have been yours if you had appeared to her in a different dress."

Coniraya tried to restore Cavillaca and the boy to their human forms. But his magic was not strong enough. He did not succeed, and he was as lonely as before. No doubt some more powerful spirits took pity upon him, for he was not alone long. The gods sent him another bride who flew down from the sky on the back of the giant condor whom he had blessed. She made him happy, so happy that he no longer had time for unpleasant practical jokes.

THE GIFT OF MANIOC

THE GOD-WHO-MADE-THE-WORLD IS KNOWN by different names in different lands. Among the Aymara Indians of Peru and Bolivia he is Pachacamac.

Not only was Pachacamac, for them, the Maker-of-All-Things, but also the Giver-of-All-Gifts. It was he who made this earth such a pleasant place in which to live. He put Inti, the sun, in the sky to give men light and warmth so that plants could grow. He gave them the sturdy llamas to carry their burdens, and the llama's cousins, the alpacas; the guanacos and the vicunas, whose soft furry skins could be used in so many ways.

To look after his good earth he trusted Pacha-Mama, the Earth Goddess, who would give the plants and the animals tender care.

Best of all the gifts of Pachacamac, many Indians thought, was manioc, the potatolike root which provided their daily bread. And it was not strange that they should have many stories about how it came to the earth. Some tell it like this.

Once—oh, it was a long, long time ago—there lived a beautiful girl, the daughter of a powerful Indian chief. She was as good as she was fair, and everyone loved her. When she walked through the forest, the birds sang more sweetly. She could lie down to sleep under a tree in the deep jungle, and no beast would harm her.

One day a certain woman who belonged to the same tribe came to the father of this good and fair maiden. She was an old woman, a wise woman, and everyone paid heed to her words.

"I have news for you, O Chief," the Wise Woman said. "News about your dear daughter. News which I will exchange for a gift from your storehouse."

"Speak, woman, speak! If indeed you have such news!" the Chief replied quickly.

"Almost I fear to speak for my news will not please you. Yet it is the truth."

"What news could you have for me about my daughter, Wise Woman, that should not please me? Speak. Do not fear. If it be the truth, no harm shall come to you. And there shall be a gift for you out of my storehouse."

"Well, then, O Chief, know that out in the forest your daughter has been married. Her husband is a handsome, young stranger, no Indian like us. His skin is as pale as the milk-white tears of the rubber tree. And pale will be the skin of the child who will be born of this marriage. A girl-child it will be, one who shall bring blessings upon all in this land."

The Chief flew into a terrible rage. He knew that this woman was wise, so wise that she could tell of things that would happen long before they took place.

Such a strange, unseemly marriage would lay shame on his roof. Even the promise of blessings which his daughter's girl-child would bring could not quiet his anger. But he remembered his promise

58

to the Wise Woman, and she went her way in peace.

Then the Chief called for his daughter. With glowering eyes and stormy voice, he questioned her thus.

"Who is this young man you have secretly wed in the deep forest?"

"I have wed no man, my father," the girl declared.

"The Wise Woman does not lie. She gives me news of your marriage to a handsome young stranger, whose skin is as white as the milky tears of the rubber tree."

"Truly, dear father, I have never seen such a man," the Chief's daughter was weeping now. "If ever I met such a one it must have been in a dream. And in a dream which I forgot before I opened my eyes."

The Chief loved his dear daughter. He wished to believe her.

"So it may have been," he said. "But if you have not spoken truly, my child, you shall die."

All went well then until, as the Wise Woman foretold, a girl-child was born to the Chief's daughter. It was a strange baby, a very strange baby to be born in an Indian hut. For the little one had a skin as white as a summer cloud. Who could have been her father save the handsome, pale stranger of whom the Wise Woman had spoken? The proud Chief flew once more into a rage, more terrible than before.

"They shall both die," he vowed, "my daughter and the pale girl-child who have brought shame upon me." And he went into his hut, and he wept bitter tears.

But during the night this Indian Chief himself had a dream. And it was a dream he remembered when he awoke. In it a handsome youth stood before him, a stranger with skin as white as the tears

59

of the rubber tree. In the dream the youth spoke, saying, "Do not punish your daughter, O Chief. Do not kill her baby. No harm has been done. No shame, only glory shall rest on the roof of your house.

"I am the son of the great Pachacamac and of Pacha-Mama, the Earth-Mother. It was I who married your daughter while she dreamed in the forest. It is I who am her husband and the father of her child, whose name shall be Mani. Forgive your daughter, O Chief! Love the child, Mani, and she will bring blessings upon all in your land."

These words of the Spirit from Heaven brought peace to the heart of the Chief. He forgave his dear daughter. Soon, like everyone else in the tribe, he had fallen under the spell of the baby girl, Mani.

Never had there been known such a child. Her skin was white as the lilies that floated on the dark forest pools. Her eyes were bright as the stars. Almost from the first, the little girl could walk and talk. From far and near people came to gaze upon her and wonder.

Then one day, when Mani was about two years old, her short life was ended. She did not seem ill. Nor did she feel pain. There was a smile on her gentle lips when her spirit floated away to join her father and her grandmother, Pacha-Mama, in the sky.

As was their custom, the Indians buried the tiny body of their beloved Mani in a small house set in the midst of a garden. A house without walls they built for her, with a roof that shielded her grave from the greatest heat of the sun. Each day they sprinkled water upon the mound of earth above her so that she would never be thirsty.

One morning a strange thing was observed. The earth mound had opened, and a curious green plant had thrust its head out of the ground. It grew and it grew before those Indians' eyes, until it became a tall bush.

"Look at those strange leaves," the people said. "See how they are shaped, just like a hand with the fingers spread open! They are like the pretty fingers and hands of our dear little Mani."

Blossoms opened on Mani's plant. Fruit formed, and the birds ate of it greedily. "The birds devour the fruit in the house of Mani, then they sing merry songs. Watch how swiftly they fly! It is as if they had had a good drink that made them happy and gay." These were the cries of wonder from the amazed onlookers.

Later on, in the crack in the small mound, someone noticed a cluster of white roots at the foot of the bush. They were long pointed roots as big around as a potato.

"Look at the roots in Mani's house," the people exclaimed. "They are pale. They are white, like Mani's skin. This plant must be the blessing which the Wise Woman foretold."

As they talked of the roots which they took from the bush, they spoke again and again the word "Mani-Hot" or "the House of Mani." And that, so the story says, is how the plant got its name, manioc.

In other dreams the Spirit of Manioc, that handsome white stranger who had wed the Chief's daughter, told the Indians how to make use of the manioc roots. He warned them that it had a poisonous juice, and that this must be squeezed out. Its pulp must be well roasted before it can be pounded to flour for making porridge and cakes, or for thickening stew.

Only one thing did the son of the Earth-Mother forget. He did not tell the people how they should plant manioc so as to raise more in their gardens. It was little Mani herself who appeared in a dream to her mother one night.

"Tell the women, dear mother, that they must cut up the stalk of my plant into very small pieces. They must put these pieces into the ground with only a light cover of soil above them. The sun should warm them. The rain should keep them moist. Then they will grow, and our people will never lack food.

So it was the chief's daughter and a little girl-child who gave these northern Indians the plant which feeds them best. And it is the women there who still tend the manioc. "The mani-hot will not come up out of the ground if it is planted by men instead of by women." That is what the Indians there say.

Do you think the men truly believe this old saying? Or do you think perhaps they are glad to lie, swinging gently in their hammocks of palm fiber, while they watch their wives do the hard work?

And preparing the manioc was hard work. The roots were soaked and grated fine. Then they were put into a long basket tube called a *tipity*. Mani herself must have told her people how to hang the tipity from a high tree branch by a loop on one end. She must have explained that a woman could sit on a pole that ran through the loop on the other end of the basket tube. Her weight would pull the meshes of the tipity tight and narrow. Then the poison juice would run out.

Dried in the sun or baked over a fire, the manioc meal was made ready for use.

But the Indian women never grumbled. They were grateful for the gift of manioc which kept hunger away from their huts.

63

THE GOLDEN GOURD

In other times, in Brazil far to the north, there once lived two brothers. One was selfish Silverio, who was rich. The other was honest Manoel, who was poor.

Why was it that two sons of the same father should have had such different luck? No one can answer that question. But there it was. Silverio had a comfortable house, broad fields, and deep forests. His clothes were of the best. Always there was more food on his table than he could eat. But Manoel had nothing to tell about. He owned only an acre of ground and a hut so bare that one scarcely would wish to use it as a cow shed.

One day poor Manoel went to his brother's house and knocked on the door.

"Silverio, my brother," he said, "I am in trouble. I need your help. On my bit of ground I never can raise enough manioc to feed my wife and my children. You have so much land you cannot use it all. Will you not lend a little to me, so that I can keep hunger out of my hut?"

Now, one would think that Silverio would have been sorry for his own brother's plight. One would think he would have been glad to loan him a small piece of good land. But, instead of really helping his brother in his distress, selfish Silverio decides to play a mean joke upon him.

"Of course, my dear brother," he said, pretending to be kind, "of course I'll spare you some land. I will not just make it a loan. I will give it to you. You shall have all of the western acres which I got from old Tomaso."

"How kind you are, Silverio! A thousand thanks! And may Heaven bless you as you deserve!" Poor Manoel wept for joy at the thought of the manioc he could raise with all this new land.

But Silverio laughed as his happy brother went away to look at his gift. The piece of land he had given him was only a wilderness. It was by far the worst of all the acres which this rich man owned. Nothing would grow upon it save sharp thistles and scrubby bushes.

"Wife! Wife!" Manoel called out when he reached his hut. "Silverio has kindly given me a piece of his land. Come with me to look at it."

"Here is something new," his wife said scornfully. "Silverio is kind? Silverio is making you a fine gift?" She shook her head doubtfully, but she went along with her husband just the same.

As they walked across their brother's meadows, the woman stopped now and then.

"Do you think this could be it?" she said when, in the distance, they saw a smooth clearing.

"No," Manoel replied. "We must go far to the west. It is the piece of land which Silverio got from old Tomaso. I shall know it by its markers."

They walked, and they walked. At last they came to the markers of the acres which Silverio had said his brother might have. And their faces fell. The ground was so rough. It was covered with prickly thistles and low scrubby bushes. It would take many a year to clear this ground enough to plant manioc here.

"Well, I can at least cut down some of the bushes," poor Manoel said, trying to comfort his wife. "We can dry them and burn them under our cooking pot."

Just then his wife gave a cry of surprise. She rushed into the thicket.

"Look, Manoel, look! What can this be? It looks like a gourd, but it is yellow like gold." She pointed to a big round golden object hanging from a low bush.

"It is shaped like a gourd," her husband said. He could not believe his own eyes. "It is the size of a huge wasp's nest. But it truly is gold, pure gold. Oh, this is good fortune! It will bring us many pesos." He almost danced in his joy.

Then his face grew doubtful.

"I forget myself, Wife," he cried. "Silverio would never have given us this land if he had known about this golden gourd. The treasure belongs to my brother. It cannot be ours."

"Silverio gave you these acres, this wilderness," his wife insisted. "This poor land is yours. Thus, whatever is found upon it also belongs to you." The woman could not help thinking of her hungry children and of how much food the golden gourd would buy for them.

Honest Manoel shook his head.

"No, my dear wife," he cried. I must first tell Silverio what we have found. Then if he says that everything on the land is ours, we can keep the gourd. We must not touch it until he gives us leave."

66

So the poor couple went off to find their rich brother.

"Silverio, we have found a golden gourd on the land which you said I might have," Manoel explained. "It hangs on a bush in a thicket, and it seems to be made of pure gold. It did not seem right that I should take it for myself without your leave."

Stingy Silverio could scarcely keep his greed from showing. "Of course that changes everything, Manoel," he said, "I cannot give away land upon which there are gourds of pure gold. You shall have a piece of woodland instead." And the greedy man hurried away to see for himself the fabulous golden fruit of his bush.

Silverio walked fast. He came at last to the very spot where Manoel and his wife had seen the golden gourd.

"It is not here," he said, looking in vain for the glint of yellow gold. "I will look elsewhere." And he plunged this way and that through the thorny thicket in search of the rich treasure.

The only thing he found, which at all resembled a gourd, was a huge wasp's nest. And this had the fierce insects crawling by the hundreds over its gray shell.

You can imagine how angry Silverio was.

"It was all a trick of Manoel's to get hold of a better piece of land," he declared. "I will get even with him. He shall see."

He lifted the wasps' nest out of the thicket. Gently, gently he handled it, so that the wasps would not sting him. Such very big ones could easily sting a man to death.

Silverio managed to get the nest into the leather sack which he brought with him for taking the golden gourd home. With the sack on his back, he made his way to the hut of his needy brother.

"Ho, Manoel!" he called out, "I bring you a gift. Shut your door

tight. Close the windows, except for one. And leave that one window open just wide enough so that I may throw the golden gourd in to you. Then you must close it tight also."

Inside Manoel's hut, there was a hurry and scurry as the happy man obeyed his brother's words. He and his wife closed the door and the windows. As they did so, the poor brother called out, "How kind you are Silverio! A thousand thanks! And may Heaven bless you just as much as you deserve to be blessed."

Even these trusting words did not soften Silverio's heart. He went on with his cruel trick. He put the neck of the leather sack in the open window and shook it, releasing the wasp's nest and the angry insects inside Manoel's hut. He himself closed the window so that none could get out.

Then he waited to hear the cries of pain of the poor people, shut up with the wasps. But to his surprise no cries came.

Inside Manoel's hut a strange happening took place. Every one of those wasps was turned into a piece of pure yellow gold. The earth floor was covered with golden coins. It took Manoel and his wife and their children, too, a long time to gather them and put them into sacks.

Outside, Silverio still waited to hear cries of distress. Once he thought he heard the clink of metal coins. But he knew that could not be.

Again he heard sounds as of people moving about. Perhaps they were trying to kill the angry wasps or to get out of their way. At last his curiosity got the better of him.

"Manoel! Brother!" he called. "What are you doing? Open your door to me!"

But a monkey does not put his paw in a jaguar's mouth twice.

Good Manoel had learned his lesson. He knew better than to tell his brother of this good fortune.

"Go away, Silverio," he called back. "Go away! Leave us alone! The wasps have done their duty. We have no further need of you."

Well, Silverio went away. It was not until much later, when the gold coins had been spent to buy some truly good land, that Manoel told of the riches which the wasps' nest had brought him.

"It was a gift from the gods," he said, "and truly Heaven blessed Silverio just as much as he deserved to be blessed, which was not at all."

All the neighbors laughed at Silverio. They loved to repeat this tale about the golden gourd which made a poor man rich and a rich man ridiculous.

THE LITTLE BLACK BOOK OF MAGIC

YOUNG MARCO LIVED LONG AGO in the South American land of
Argentina. At least, the old people there say that he did. They
remember how he found the wizard's little black book of magic.
They liked to tell about the exciting adventures it brought him.

In those ancient times, people talked a great deal about wizards
and their magic. There was no way of knowing just who might
be a wizard. With his magic a wizard could make himself look
like an Argentine gaucho, an ordinary cowboy riding over the
grassy plains. Or he could change himself into a horse, a rooster,
a fish, or a bird.

One could never be sure, either, whether the spirit inside one
of these strange forms was good or bad. Even the wickedest wizard
of all, the Devil himself, was on the earth then.

There is a wizard in this story. There is also a brave youth who
got the best of him.

This clever youth, Marco, was the youngest son of a very poor
family. He lived with his crippled father and his mother and his
two brothers in a miserable rancho hut.

Bad luck, too, dwelt under that roof. Marco and his brothers, Lino and Luis, often were hungry. Their ponchos were ragged. Their shabby shirts were not always clean for they had only one each.

It was their ragged clothing that kept Lino and Luis from going to school when they were younger. At least they told everyone that was the reason. Their schoolteacher said it was more because they were lazy.

Like his brothers, Marco also wore ragged clothes. But he went to school just the same. He studied hard, and he learned how to read.

Well, the day came when these three brothers were almost grown-up. They were quite old enough to earn money to help their poor parents. So together they set forth. They went to every rancho in their part of the grass lands of the Argentine pampas. To the big ranchos, and to the small ones they went. But they found no work. Not even one peso did they bring home.

Now and then friends brought small gifts of beef and cornmeal and the good tea called mate. But most of the time there was almost nothing to eat or drink in their poor hut. Things went from bad to worse.

Then one day, Lino, the oldest brother, said, "I will go farther from home, out into the wide world. Somewhere there, surely, I can find work. Perhaps I shall even become rich."

His father shook his head. He was not so sure. Lino had a good heart, but he truly was lazy. "Go, my son," said the lame man. "Try your luck in the wide world. And may the Good God keep the wicked spirits away from you."

Lino walked far through the pampas grass. But nowhere did

73

he find riches to take back to his parents. Indeed, often he had no more food in his stomach than he had had at home. He was feeling sorry and sad when he turned around.

But on his way back to his hut, he came upon a long, low rancho almost hidden in the tall pampas grass. At his knock, a strange-looking man opened the door. He was very tall, very thin, and his skin was dead white. His fierce eyes shone like two coals of bright fire, and he wore a little goat's beard.

Instead of a gaucho's usual loose shirt and baggy breeches, the Pale Man had on a long black coat and tight trousers like those seen in a city. A red cap was fitted tightly over his skull.

Lino was frightened by his eerie appearance, but he managed to say politely, "Señor, I look for work. I must earn a few pesos to buy food for my hungry parents."

"Well, there is work to be done here," the Pale Man replied. "But first I must ask whether you know how to read."

Lino's heart sank. Now he would surely be turned away.

"Alas, no, señor," he said. "I never had clothes fit for going to school."

To his surprise, however, the Pale Man seemed pleased.

"Good! Good!" he said. "Come in, young fellow, and I'll put you to work. Tomorrow I go away on a journey. You shall mind my rancho during the two days I shall be away. You shall feed my cows and my horses. And there is even more important work for you to do." He led Lino into three gloomy rooms in one end of the rancho. Each one was filled with piles and piles of old books.

"These musty rooms are to be aired and cleaned," he said. "So these books all are to be moved to the other end of the rancho. You must carry them there before I come back." And he rode away.

Now lazy Lino was not accustomed to this kind of work. And there were a great many books. By twos and by threes, he slowly picked them up. He had moved only half of those in the first room when his master came home.

"Go along, lazy fellow." His employer was cross. "Here is your pay!" And he threw a gold coin into Lino's old hat.

"Oh, that Pale Man was angry. I was afraid," Lino told his family, "but then he gave me the gold coin which bought this good beef for our supper."

As they sat round the table, Marco, the youngest of the three brothers, said, "That strange man must be a wizard. He could be the same wizard which caused our father's fall from his horse that broke his back." Then he added thoughtfully, "But, Lino, why did he say 'Good!' when you told him you could not read."

Neither Lino nor any other one at the table could think of a reason.

"It does not really matter," Luis, the middle brother, declared. "The man gave you a gold coin. Perhaps he will hire me, since I, too, cannot read. Perhaps he will give me another gold coin. I will go to his rancho."

All happened with Luis as it had with Lino. When he was asked if he could read, he made the same answer. "Alas, no, Señor. I never had clothes fit for going to school." So he was put to work, and his strange master went off on his journey.

Luis worked a little faster than Lino. He carried a few more books on each trip to the other end of the rancho. But he was only starting to work in the second room when the Pale Man came home.

"Go, lazybones!" he shouted. "You have done little better than the fellow who came here just a few days ago." His dark, angry eyes burned more fiercely than ever. Luis, too, was afraid when his master seized him by the arm and pushed him out of the door. "Here is your pay!" The Pale Man threw two golden coins down on the ground beside him.

These bought food for many days for the family, but even though no one was hungry now, young Marco declared that he wanted to seek out the rancho of this strange man whom he suspected of being a wizard.

His brothers laughed.

"How shall you who are younger do better than we?" Luis cried.

"The Pale Man will not hire you," Lino said. "You know how to read."

Marco went in spite of their warnings. And the strange rancho owner with the goat's beard and the fiery eyes opened the door to his knock.

"Yes, there is work here," he said for a third time. "But first tell me, young fellow, do you know how to read?"

Marco had thought well how he should answer, and he replied, "Look at my ragged shirt, Señor. Who would go to school in clothing like mine?"

Of course, this did not really answer the question, but the Pale Man seemed satisfied.

"Well then, come in," he said. "Mind my house, feed my animals, and move all these books while I am away."

As soon as his employer was out of sight, Marco explored the gloomy house. How eerie it was! How dark! How silent and big! Prickles of fear ran down his spine. But he somehow found courage to go to work.

76

He moved the books quickly. At the end of the first day he had emptied the second room. But in the third chamber he shook his head in dismay. There were twice as many books here as in the two other rooms together. He could never finish this task in time. So he stopped to read a page here and there in each volume he picked up.

In the second pile he came upon a little black book. It was old, very old, almost falling apart, and as Marco read its yellow pages, he gave an excited cry.

"This is a book of magic!" He spoke aloud. "I guessed right. The Pale Man is a wizard, the same wicked wizard who caused my father's fall from his horse.

"I do not know if this magic book is rightfully his, for there are other names written inside its cover," he continued, "but I shall take it away with me to protect myself and my family from more of his mischief. With this little black book of magic, I shall beat this wicked devil at his own game."

In his new-found treasure Marco found the words he needed to speak to move all the books in the wink of an eye. From it he also learned the wizard's trick of changing himself from one form to another. He tried this out by turning himself into a mouse. Then he said other magic words and lo, he was a dog. The spells worked for him as they, no doubt, worked for a real wizard.

The owner of the rancho was surprised when he came home that evening. His cows had been milked. His pigs had been fed. His horses had been watered. And every book had been moved.

"Hi-yi!" cried the Pale Man. "How can this be? However did you manage to move all the books?"

"They are moved, Señor. You can see that for yourself." Marco's words could not be denied, and the wizard did not know quite what to do. He was a little afraid of this youth who had completed a humanly impossible task.

"You shall be well paid," he said to Marco. And the youth replied pleasantly, "Pay me what you please, Señor. I shall be content." He did not say that he had already taken his pay in the little black book of magic which lay deep in his trousers' pocket.

"The brown horse in my barn shall carry you home, Marco," the wizard said then. "Load my white mule with these three bags of gold coins. And when you reach your rancho, let the beasts go free to find their own way back to me."

Marco was too clever to believe that the wizard was as generous as he seemed. He was sure there was a trick of some kind in the offer. He went around behind the rancho while he searched in the book of magic to find out what he should do.

From it he learned that the horse and the mule were evil spirits like their owner. So when he came to the barn, he was not surprised to find the brown horse snorting and rearing. He barely escaped being kicked to his death by the white mule.

"Beware of the Good God in Heaven, you devils!" he shouted.

At once the animals were quiet. The brown horse allowed himself to be saddled. The white mule did not move while the heavy bags of gold were put on his back. And Marco went home in triumph.

With the wizard's gold, Marco bought a better rancho for his family. Now they could have horses and cows. They could all buy new clothes in the city. Good luck now lived under their roof.

"But we must not be careless," he warned his father. "The wizard will try his best to recover his little black book of magic.

Some Sunday he will ride here in the form of a gaucho. Dressed as a cowboy, he will ask for a race, and you must agree." This he had discovered by repeating a magic spell which told him what was to happen.

"I shall change myself into an old nag, a broken-down horse that can scarcely stand on his feet. You shall offer me for the race, my father. When he sees the weak creature I shall be, the wizard will bet many gold coins on our race. But I shall win. Then he will wish to buy your old nag. Sell me, but take care, oh, take good care to take off my bridle before you give me up to him."

As Marco foretold, he won the race with the wizard's horse. The gold coins were paid, ten for winning the race and twenty as a purchase price for the nag. But, alas, Marco's father thought only of the gold coins he was getting. He forgot to take off Marco's bridle.

The wicked wizard stuck his sharp spurs into the sides of the aged horse. He beat it with his whip. His knowledge of spells told him that this nag was Marco, the youth who had taken away his little black book of magic.

Now, on his way home, the wizard stopped at the rancho of one of his evil friends. He tied the nag to a tree on the edge of a lake and went into the house.

A passing gaucho saw the weary old horse. The animal drooped, and panted for water. And the cowboy was sorry for it. He took off its bridle so that it might drink from the lake.

With a scream of anger, the wizard came running out of the rancho. But even more quickly Marco, the nag, jumped into the lake.

Once in the water, Marco spoke magic words that changed his

form of a horse into that of a fish. He swam quickly away.

The wizard, however, turned himself into a shark. And he swam even faster. When Marco reached the other shore of the lake, the devil-shark was close on his tail.

"Let me now be a deer!" Marco called out, and he bounded away over the pampas. Loud barking behind told him that the wizard now was a swift hunting hound which could outrun any deer.

Only a bird in the air is safe from a hound, he thought. So he became a dove, flying high into the sky. A fierce hawk attacked him there, and of course this, too, was the wizard.

Before the hawk could kill the dove, Marco changed into a wee hummingbird so that he could hide himself under the wing of an eagle that was flying nearby. But the wizard now took on the form of a mighty condor, the biggest of birds. Flapping its great wings, the condor flew at the eagle.

High above the pampas the two birds fought fiercely. Then they swooped down over a fine house, Marco saw that a narrow window was open in a tower room. Still in his hummingbird form, he dropped from under the eagle's wing into the shelter of the tower.

The condor pursued the tiny creature, but the window was hardly more than a slit in the wall. The great bird could not follow it inside the tower.

Marco had just time to take on his own form once more. With a loud voice he shouted, "Beware of the Good God in Heaven who protects me!" And the condor, in terror, flew swiftly away.

All this happened before the eyes of Rosa, the young daughter of the owner of this fine house. Marco thought he had never seen so beautiful a girl. It was not strange that she herself was pleased with such a brave young man. Nor that she should appeal to him for help.

"My father keeps me shut up in this tower," Rosa explained. "I do not blame him. He is only trying to keep me safe from a wicked wizard who wants me for his bride. My father is deeply in debt to this evil one who holds him in his power. Oh, good young stranger, help me to escape."

Marco remembered the spell which told of future happenings. And he said, "You shall buy your freedom from this devil with your jewels, dear Rosa. Give him your necklace and your bracelets. Give him all your rings except for one small golden circlet which you will wear on a chain round your neck. That small golden ring will be I myself, Marco, and this is what you must do with it."

The girl listened well. And she followed Marco's instructions to the smallest detail.

When the wizard came courting her, she poured a heap of gold and bright gems on a table before him. And she begged him to take them to pay her father's debts.

"These are not all of your treasures," the wicked wizard cried. "I must have also the little gold ring on that chain round your neck." His magic was strong. He knew the ring was Marco.

Rosa tossed the ring on the table as she had been instructed. It rolled off and as it fell to the floor it became a golden pomegranate which burst open and scattered its bright seeds hither and yon.

In an instant, the wizard changed himself into a rooster. He pecked at the seeds. He ate each one in sight. And he crowed, "Now at last I have the best of you, Marco!"

But one of the pomegranate seeds had fallen close to Rosa's feet. Luckily this seed was Marco, and as she pushed it under the table, he changed himself into a fox. With a leap, the fox sprang upon the rooster. He killed it even before it had finished its crowing.

"We are both safe now, dear Rosa," Marco said to the daughter of the rich man. He was standing before her in his own person, handsome and tall.

"Your father now is free from the power of the wizard," he said, taking her hand. "As my reward I shall ask him for permission to marry you, if you will only consent. I shall take you away to a fine house of our own. And with my little black book of magic, this devil shall never enter our door. No, not even if he should come back from the Other World in the form of a tall, thin man with a dead-white face, fiery eyes, and a little goat's beard."

Rosa said, "Yes," and her father gave his permission.

So the old people in Argentina tell the story of Marco and the little black book of magic. They say the two young people lived happily together for the rest of their lives.

If there is a lesson to be learned from this tale, one must compare Marco's adventures with those of his lazy brothers, Lino and Luis. This will show, surely, that it pays for a boy to go to school and learn how to read.

CLEVER CARMELITA

THIS HAPPENED, people say, in a Chilean town, which had a young Spanish Governor. It was long ago, but also it was after the conquerors from over the sea began ruling the land. This young Governor, whose name may well have been Don Pedro, set great store by cleverness. He himself had the sharpest mind in all the land. Not one of his counselors could get the best of him in a matching of wits.

Now Don Pedro was not married. When people suggested that he should take a wife, he would always reply, "I shall wed only a girl who is as clever as I am. Find me such a one, and you shall have your wedding feast."

The people of that city shook their heads. There were plenty of beautiful girls to be had—Spanish girls and daughters of Indian Chiefs. But how would they ever discover one half as clever as their young Governor, when no man was a match for him?

Don Pedro liked a joke. When he was out riding, he often reined in his horse to ask a trick question of some simple girl—just for the fun of seeing her eyes grow wide and her jaw drop, as she stood speechless before him.

83

One day as he walked his horse through a village just outside the city, he came upon a girl who was watering a basil plant near the gate of her garden. The garden belonged to a well-to-do man who had three pretty daughters. On this afternoon it was Teresa, the oldest, who was taking her turn with the watering.

Don Pedro greeted her with this little verse.

> *Good day, fair maid, 'tis good to see,*
> *A plant cared for so tenderly.*
> *Upon its stalk, pray tell to me,*
> *How many small green leaves there be.*

At these words of the handsome young Governor, the girl's face grew red. She hung her head, and she rushed into her house. Of course she did not know how many leaves the basil plant had. And she could not think what to reply.

The next time the young horseman came past the garden, the middle sister, Floriana, was watering the basil plant. Again the joking Don Pedro put the same question. And like Teresa, Floriana stammered and blushed and ran into the house.

But when the young man stopped at this garden gate a third time, it was Carmelita, the youngest daughter of the family, who was tending the green plant. She was as fair as her sisters, and she was known all through the neighborhood for her clever wit.

Carmelita did not hang her head when Don Pedro called out teasingly:

> *Good day, fair maid, 'tis good to see,*
> *A plant cared for so tenderly.*
> *Upon its stalk, pray tell to me,*
> *How many small green leaves there be?*

No, Carmelita did not blush. She did not run indoors to hide.

Instead she looked up at the young man on his prancing horse, and, using a verse, just as he had, she said:

> *First, do you who question me,*
> *Tell how many fish swim in the sea?*

This time it was Don Pedro who was silent. He did not know how he could answer her question. He rode away, half angry and half pleased with the clever girl.

"I'll get the best of her another time," he promised himself. And he thought, and he thought until he had a plan that was sure to embarrass her.

When he reached home, the young Governor called for the head cook in his household. This was an old man, both ugly and blind.

"Tomorrow," he gave the order, "you must dress yourself like a street cake-seller. Take a basket of hot, fried cakes on your arm. Go to this house of the three sisters. I want you to sell your cakes to Carmelita, the youngest one. Take no money from her! See that she pays you with a kiss instead! And take care that you do not say it was I who sent you."

"Cakes for sale! Hot fried cakes for sale! Who'll buy my cakes!"

The two older sisters heard the cake-seller's call. They ran to the door to answer his knock.

"We have no money to buy your hot cakes, old man," Teresa said regretfully. "But our youngest sister, Carmelita, who is washing clothes in the brook—she always has pesos in her apron pocket. Perhaps she will buy."

"Cakes for sale! Hot fried cakes for sale! Who'll buy my cakes?"

Carmelita rose from her knees on the bank of the brook when she heard this tempting call. She put her hand in her apron pocket to take out a coin to give to him.

"No, *niña*," said the old cake-seller. "I do not sell these good, hot, fried cakes for money. I sell only for kisses."

"For kisses, indeed! Only for kisses! Then you can just take them away from here." Carmelita gave a ringing laugh at the thought that she would ever kiss such an ugly old man.

"Why not kisses, my pretty one? What is a kiss? And for a harmless old man like me? Besides who would know? We are hidden here by the brook? I myself—I am blind. Even I could not see you. And my cakes—they are very hot and very good."

The hot fried cakes smelled so good that they made Carmelita's mouth water. So she gave the old man a fleeting kiss for each one in his basket. Then she ran home to share the feast with her two sisters.

Next day the young Governor rode past the house of the three sisters once more. Carmelita was near the garden gate, and the young horseman stopped.

> *Good day, fair maid, 'tis good to see,*
> *A plant cared for so tenderly.*
> *Upon its stalk, pray tell to me,*
> *How many small green leaves there be.*

Carmelita laughed. This was a good game. As before she gave him back her own verse:

> *First, do you who question me,*
> *Tell how many fish swim in the sea.*

Now the young man had another verse in reply. With twinkling eyes and teasing voice, and watching the girl's pretty face, he said:

> *Ho, Carmelita, down by the brook,*
> *How many times did you kiss my cook?*

87

Then Carmelita's cheeks burned like fire. She shook her head, and speechless, she ran into the house and slammed the door. She was angry. And she vowed that she would get even with this proud young man who had played such a trick to embarrass her.

For weeks Carmelita thought of nothing else but Don Pedro. Each day she had a new idea, but none seemed to please her. Then one afternoon, she learned that the young man had fallen ill.

"He is not very sick," people said. "But he greatly fears he will die."

Carmelita dressed herself in a gray wig and a long robe, so as to resemble Saint Anthony. Leading a fat pig, as the good saint was known to do, she made her way to the Governor's house.

"Saint Anthony! Saint Anthony!" Don Pedro's servants fell on their knees when they saw the familiar bent figure leading the pig. And they took these two travelers at once to the room where Don Pedro lay on his couch.

"The Good God has sent me to you, my poor friend." Carmelita's voice sounded just like that of a man. "You have been faithful. You have not forgotten your daily prayers. Now that you are about to die, I come to help you get ready."

"Good Saint Anthony, I beg you. I am too young to die. Help me to live instead."

The false saint's head was bowed. No words came for a moment. Then she spoke slowly.

"God loves the meek, my son. Show him that your heart is humble. Perhaps then he will be pleased and will grant you longer to live.

"This poor creature by my side is my friend and companion. Yet it is only a pig, one of the lowliest of God's creatures. Show your

88

meekness by treating it as your brother. For each kiss you give my pig, I will pray that the good God grant you one more year of life."

The young man was eager to live. He leapt up from his couch, and he pressed a full hundred kisses on the pig's bristly head. Then still bending over, in her saint's disguise, Carmelita led the animal away.

Of course Don Pedro soon was well again. In truth, he had never been very sick. On the first day he could mount his horse, he rode past the house of the fair Carmelita. Though he would not yet admit it, he had fallen in love with this girl who was so pretty and so clever.

> *Good day, fair maid, again I see,*
> *Your plant is cared for tenderly.*
> *Upon its stalk, pray tell to me,*
> *How many small green leaves there be.*

Carmelita laughed merrily as their game began again. She had a surprise for this joker! But first she replied as before.

> *First, do you who question me,*
> *Tell how many fish swim in the sea.*

Pleased to think he was to have the last word in teasing the girl, Don Pedro repeated his rhyme.

> *Ho, Carmelita, down by the brook,*
> *How many times did you kiss my cook?*

But this was not the last word. Ah, no! To the young man's great surprise, Carmelita tossed her head and cried gaily:

> *A saint can be made with robe and wig,*
> *How many times did you kiss my pig?*

Don Pedro laughed until his sides ached. This witty girl had beaten him at his own game. He called his counselors together and said, "At last I have found a pretty girl who is as clever as I. I shall make Carmelita, from the House of the Three Sisters, my beloved bride."

Clever Carmelita consented to marry the young Governor of her land. But first she made him promise that when her turn came to die, he would grant her one last request. She had him put it in writing, too, so that it could not be forgotten.

The people of that part of Chile loved their Governor's good, clever, young wife. She helped them when they were in trouble. When their ruler was unjust, as sometimes all rulers are, she showed them how to change his mind. Often this made Don Pedro angry. But he loved Carmelita, and he always forgave her. That is, he did until the affair of the kitten.

One day there strayed into the Governor's garden, a kitten which belonged to a woman who lived close by. The playful little cat pleased Don Pedro. He asked the woman to sell him the kitten. But she would not. Nor would she give it to him.

Now rulers like to have their own way. And this one was determined he would have that kitten. He declared it was really his own already, that the woman had stolen it.

"Come here tomorrow, woman," he said, "I will prove before all the neighbors that this kitten was born to a cat of my household. You shall bring your mother-cat. I'll produce my own cat. We shall let the kitten itself choose between the two of them."

All the Governor's servants, his counselors, and the neighbors were gathered in the hall of Don Pedro's house. The woman's mother-cat was placed on one side of the room. A cat from the Governor's kitchen was set down on the other side. And the kitten was put midway between them.

90

Now during the night, Don Pedro had smeared catnip on the fur of his kitchen cat. The kitten at once smelled its delightful odor. At once it ran to sniff the sides of the strange cat from the Governor's kitchen. It began to lick the catnip off that cat's fur.

"You see," cried Don Pedro. "This kitten knows its own mother. It remembers the one who gave it its milk. That proves it belongs to the cat in my house." And he smiled. He was well pleased at the success of his plan. If his conscience troubled him, he thought I will pay the woman well, or I'll find another pet for her.

But just then Carmelita whispered into the ear of the kitten's true owner. The two fell to laughing as if they never would stop. Then the woman stepped forward. She picked up her kitten in one hand and its mother in the other.

"Strange indeed that would be, O Governor," she said. "Never before has a tomcat been known to have a kitten. Always, so I have been told, it is a mother-cat not a father-cat that gives milk. And your cat is a tom, not a tabby."

How the counselors and the neighbors and the servants laughed then! And how angry was the young man who had caused their mirth!

When the woman had taken her cat away, he turned to his wife in a great rage.

"This is too much," he stormed. "You have made me the laughing stock of this land. You have gone too far. This time you shall die." He was so angry that the pleas of all the people could not make Don Pedro pardon their beloved Carmelita.

"So be it my husband. I am ready to die," Carmelita agreed. "But remember, you promised to grant me one last request when this moment came. Here is my wish." She wrote a single sentence upon a piece of white paper and put it into his hands.

The anger now was gone from his face. He looked almost as if would like to take back his cruel words. Then he read what his clever Carmelita had written.

He burst out into a loud laugh. And he took her in his arms. For her sentence was this.

My last wish is that my dear husband shall die at the same moment as I.

Carmelita had won again. There was nothing he could do but grant her his pardon. For of course, Don Pedro had no idea of dying himself.

THE HAIRY MAN FROM THE FOREST

A CURUPIRA WAS A small, brown, hairy man who lived in the forests along the great Amazon River. People of ancient times said his feet were set upon his legs with the toes turned to the back. The footprints he made always pointed in the other direction from the one he took through the jungle. Thus his enemies never could find him when they tried to follow his tracks.

Some people said that the curupira was really only a large monkey, a kind of orangutan, with big ears and green teeth. Others declared he was truly like a man whose small body was covered with rough brown hair.

With their shaggy wives and children, the curupiras lived far, far back in the jungle where men seldom went. His home was in the trees, and trees were his special care. No Indian boy of those times dared cut into the bark of the curupira's treasures. He believed that the small hairy man would lead him off into the bushes until he was lost and could never find his way home again.

Men of those ancient times—and women too—said they had heard the sound of the curupira beating on the tree roots that grow out of the ground. They explained that the hairy man was testing them with his stone club to make sure they were firm enough to hold the trees steady in the high winds of a storm.

93

Women often saw the backward footprints of the curupira in their garden patches. These proved that it was the hairy ones who had dug up the manioc roots. People of the long ago did not like the curupira. They were afraid of him, too, like Upar's wife in this tale.

Upar was a hunter whose hut stood on a riverbank. There he lived with his wife and his little son, whom he loved dearly.

One afternoon this hunter was away from home, looking for turtles, when he heard a strange sound off to one side in the bushes. The man must have forgotten all about curupiras, or he would never have stepped out of the trail to find out what the sound was.

Again and again he heard it in the thickets beyond. On and on he went, farther and farther into the jungle. At last he was lost. Night came. There was nothing for him to do but to lie down at the foot of a tree and go to sleep.

While Upar slept, the curupira who had led him off the trail into the woods, took his clothes away. This hairy man put them on. He made himself look just like the hunter. He even carried the man's bow and arrows in his hands so that Upar's wife should not guess that he was not her husband.

The woman had waited for Upar and their supper was ready when the curupira came to the hut. In the dim light of the evening, she did not look closely at him when he put the bow and arrows in the corner. She just set the parrot stew she had cooked out on a mat.

The hairy man and the little boy sat down on the ground and ate a good meal. Then the false husband stretched himself out in Upar's hammock. The boy climbed in with him, as he always did with his father, and they both fell asleep.

94

But the moon shone on the hammock, and in its bright light, Upar's wife soon discovered that this man was not her husband. By the shaggy hair on his body, she was sure he was a curupira. And she knew she must run away from her hut just as fast as she could.

Gently she lifted her child out of the hammock. In his place, on the arm of the sleeping curupira, she laid a small log of wood. Then, with the child riding upon her hip, she ran through the forest.

It was not long before the curupira awoke. When he saw the stick of wood on his arm, he knew he had been tricked. He jumped out of the hammock and sped down the jungle path, calling, "Woman! Oh, Woman!" just as the husband, Upar, was wont to do.

"Woman! Oh Woman, where are you?" the curupira cried loudly.

Upar's wife heard him. Soon she saw him in the moonlight that sifted down through the tree branches.

"Get under this bush. Do not make a sound. We must hide from the hairy one," the woman warned her small boy. She lay close to the child, scarcely daring to breathe, lest the curupira hear her.

Now, the curupira was not noted for having quick wits. Even though a tattletale bird on a branch overhead called out three times, the hairy man did not guess it was trying to tell him that the woman was hiding nearby. He only ran faster on down the trail.

When she thought it was safe, Upar's wife took the child astride her hip again. And she ran in another direction. She ran and she ran, until at last she came to a hollow tree. At its foot there sat a big frog, smearing some thick gum over its trunk.

"Good frog," cried the woman, "save me from the curupira! Oh, save me, dear frog."

"I will save you, mother," the frog replied. "You and your child shall hide in this hollow tree. You can climb high, high inside it, up amid its green branches. And I will block up its entrance with gum. The curupira cannot get at you there."

Somehow or other, the curupira found out that he had lost the trail of the woman. He ran back to the tree where she was hiding.

"Is Upar's wife here?" the hairy man asked the frog. "Where is she hiding?" But the frog only gave forth its usual hoarse evening call, and went on with his work, smearing the tree trunk with gum.

"She is here. I know it." The angry curupira started to climb the tree so that he could look down into its trunk from above. When he had reached a high branch, the frog pulled the gum quickly out of the tree opening, and Upar's wife ran out.

The hairy man tried to follow her, but his feet were held fast by the sticky gum on the tree trunk. It was not until she was far, far away that he was able to pull himself free.

When he could not find the woman, the curupira went back to the place where he had left the sleeping hunter. He laid Upar's clothes down beside him. Then he beat on the roots of a nearby tree until the man awoke.

"What are you doing here, Friend?" the curupira asked innocently.

"Last evening I lost my way in the jungle. I had to sleep here until the morning light came to show me the way home."

"Well, this is my woodland," the hairy man declared fiercely. "You have no right to spend the night here. You must pay me for sleeping under my tree. I am hungry. You shall give me a piece of your heart to eat."

Now, as luck would have it, the hunter had killed a big monkey just the day before, and he had its heart still in his hunting bag. While the curupira was not looking, he took out his knife, and he cut off a piece of the monkey heart.

One must remember that a curupira was not very bright. He was surprised that a man would give him a piece of his heart without any fuss. He ate the bit of monkey heart which Upar handed him, and he found it good.

"I like the taste of your heart, Friend," he said to Upar. "Give me some more! Give me the whole of it. Then you shall go free."

Upar gave the curupira the rest of the monkey heart, and the small brown man ate it, believing it came from the hunter's own body.

The hunter, of course, had guessed that the small shaggy man before him was one of the hated curupiras. And he thought of a plan by which he might get rid of this one, once and for all.

"I have given you my heart, brother," he cried. "Now you give me yours."

"If this hunter can cut out his heart without hurt or harm, why then so can I," the stupid creature said to himself. And he spoke aloud. "Well, lend me your knife, hunter!" And he slashed his side open.

Of course, the knife in his heart killed the curupira. He fell dead at the feet of the clever Upar.

It was quiet and peaceful after that along Upar's part of the riverbank. No one made strange sounds in the bushes to lead him astray. No longer were the manioc roots in his clearing dug up during the night. His wife had no more fear that the hairy one would come to her hut to carry her off.

So it would have been for always if Upar had not remembered

98

that the curupira had bright green teeth.

"What beautiful beads that hairy man's bright green teeth would make!" he said to his wife one day. "What a fine necklace I should have if I should take the teeth from the skull of the dead curupira.

Upar's wife begged her husband to leave the curupira alone. But he would not listen.

When he came to the tree under which he had spent the night, he found, at its foot, the dry skeleton of the small hairy man of the forest. It lay where it had fallen, and the green teeth shone like green Amazon gems.

The man lifted his stone axe. With one blow he struck at the curupira's jaw. But the teeth did not fly out as he had expected. Instead to his great surprise, the skeleton disappeared. In its place the curupira rose from the ground, alive and well again.

"Oh, ho," the hairy man yawned. "I have had a good sleep. Thank you, my friend. Thank you for waking me. It is high time I went back to my wife and my children."

Perhaps the stupid curupira had forgotten how this hunter had tricked him. Or perhaps he was not always so wicked as the Indians of ancient times said he was. For now he seemed to feel grateful to Upar for the blow that had awakened him from the sleep of death.

"Take this arrow, my friend," the curupira said. "It is an arrow that cannot miss. With it your dinner pot need never be empty."

And so it was. Upar killed every monkey and every fish towards which he sent the magic arrow. He brought in game from the jungle such as he had never taken before. And not once again did the hairy man from the forest raid his manioc patch or frighten his wife.

THE WOMAN TRIBE

Francisco de Orellana, the great Spanish explorer of Brazil's mighty Amazon River, kept a diary as he sailed up the unknown stream. And in it he told strange tales of a tribe of fierce Indian women who lived by themselves, far, far up its course. "The Country of the Woman Tribe," was the name the river Indians gave to that place.

Orellana wrote that he himself had seen them, and he described them like this:

They are tall, very strong, with long hair twisted over their heads, skins around their waists, and bows and arrows in their hands. They fight on the battle front, like so many captains, and one of them is as good as any ten men.

The idea of such women was not new to Orellana. He had heard of others like them in tales from ancient Greece. Those warrior-women were called Amazons. So Orellana used that name also for this South American "Woman Tribe." He referred to the great river he was exploring, as the "River of the Amazons."

Perhaps there were no such creatures at all. Perhaps they were actually men. The Indians did not have beards as Spanish men do.

100

They left their hair long. Beads and bright ornaments were hung round their necks. The skins they wore about their bodies looked like women's skirts. It would have been easy for strangers to have mistaken them for women.

But all along the river, tales of the Woman Tribe came to the ears of Orellana. It is almost certain he believed them.

The Indians said the women lived on the branch of the big river, which was called the Jamundá. They tilled their land well, without help from any man. Their crops gave them all the grain they could eat. There was gold in their treasure house. But no man dared try to take their treasures away from them. The Woman Tribe was too fierce.

It was long, long ago that these women went off to live by themselves. As the Indians told it to Orellana, they came from a part of the land where the men were hard masters. They ordered their wives about. They made them work from morning until night. Few kind words did those women hear from their husbands' lips. At times the men even beat them.

So sad and so cruel was their lot, that at last the women could stand it no longer. They packed their belongings. They took their fair share of the arrows and spears, the blowguns and fishing nets. And in their husbands' dugout canoes, they fled far up the river.

The news that the women were gone spread like wildfire. And the men rushed to follow them. Of that one may be sure. They leaped into other boats. They paddled as fast as they could. When they came to the place where the women had landed, they pulled their canoes up onto the riverbank and ran over the land.

Some powerful goddess must have been angry at the cruel way in which the poor women had been treated. She must have come to the aid of her fleeing sisters. For bushes and vines were suddenly tangled behind them, hiding the path they had taken. It took their pursuers a long time to cut these thickets away.

When at last the men could go forward, a band of roaring jaguars appeared. Indeed, there were so many that they seemed like a fierce animal army. More time was lost. Many spears were thrown before all those wild beasts were driven away.

Next, howling monkeys, in trees over the men's heads, threw down great coconuts on their heads. Oh, they had a hard journey, and it was many days before they reached the clearing where their wives had decided to set up their homes.

The women must have felt sorry for their panting husbands when at last they arrived. Perhaps, indeed, they still loved their men, for they allowed them to stay for a while. But they would not go back with them.

"No," said the women. "From now on we are our own masters. We shall live here in this new land, this land we have chosen for ours. You may visit us once a year. And you may stay for a month. Then you must go away again. Of the children that are born to us, you will take only the boys. We shall keep the girls here."

So it was that these fearless wives were known all through the river country as "The Women-Who-Live-Alone." They ruled their own land. They fought their own wars. Some say they even conquered parts of the land where there were men, and that they drove them out. One Spanish traveler of those early times swore he saw, with his own eyes, a battle between the fierce warrior-women and Indian men. He said that the women easily won.

Each year, when the time came for the visit of their husbands, the women were busy for days making ready a feast. They met the men's boats at the riverbank, and there was laughing and singing when they led their guests to their huts. So long as the men stayed, their wives fed them well. And when they went away at the end of the month, the women gave them rich gifts.

Of all these gifts, the most precious were the little green stones which brought such good luck. These lucky stones were no more than three inches long. They could heal pain. They could cure the bite of a poisonous snake. The men strung them on cords and wore them as charms to keep evil spirits away.

Some of the little green Amazon stones had the shape of a fish. Others were like different birds and beasts. They were as clear and as green as the young jungle leaves. And, like precious jade, they were smooth and oily to touch.

"Where can we find more of these lucky stones?" Many a man asked this question of his wife. But she would not tell the secret.

The Indians said it was the goddess of their Moon Mirror Lake who protected this Woman Tribe. They were sure it was she who fashioned the little lucky stones out of the green clay from the lake's bottom.

"Mirror of the Moon," was a good name for this lake. For in its dark waters, the bright face of the moon could be seen, as in a looking glass.

At the time of the full moon, the Amazon women dived into its clear water. They swam and they played about as though they were children. When they came out again, they gave thanks to their goddess and praise to the moon for its heavenly light. Out of the dark lake the Spirit came to them. And into the hand of each one she put a little green stone.

The Spirit of the Amazon Stones shaped the green pebbles with

103

her own fairy fingers, they said. Far down under the water, she gave them their forms. As soon as they came out into the warm upper air, the soft clay shapes grew hard. And shut up inside them was some of their Spirit's own magic power.

People along the great river, in ancient times, believed in the luck of the little green stones. The wives of Indian Chiefs wore them like jewels around their necks. Warriors carried them into battle. And the Spanish explorers bought the stones from the Indians for their own protection.

It seems strange that these women did not want to keep the baby boys who were born to them. But it was the law of their land. No boy, nor man could stay long in their huts. Many a mother must have wept when she saw her baby son float away, out of her sight, in his father's canoe. There was a story about one such who loved her boy-child so dearly that she could not let him go.

The woman's name could have been Ica, and that of her child could have been Pahy Tuna. At least that is how they were called in the ancient Indian tale.

Pahy Tuna was weak and sick from the moment he came into the world. He was ugly, too, with a rough, bumpy skin and a crooked body. So ugly was this baby that his mother wept over him. But she loved him all the more.

"Who would ever care for a child so sick and so ugly as my Pahy Tuna?" she asked herself. "Even his father would let him die. I must keep him with me. I will find some place to hide him."

Ica, the mother of Pahy Tuna, knew she would be punished if it was discovered that she had broken the law, and kept her boy in her hut. So she hid the sick child in a cave in the deep forest. She told all her neighbors that Pahy Tuna had died.

104

Each day the poor mother crept secretly into the woods to tend her hidden baby. She cared for him so tenderly that he grew well and strong. Only his skin was still rough and bumpy. His body was still crooked. She did not know how to cure this, but one day when she was squeezing the poisonous juice out of the manioc pulp, she had an idea. It came to her as she looked at the tipity, the basketlike tube which she was using.

I put the manioc pulp into the tipity, she thought. Then I pull its meshes tight. And the poison runs out. What if I should try this with Pahy Tuna? Perhaps I could squeeze the poison out of his body, too. Perhaps the tipity could make his crooked body straight.

Ica could not get this idea out of her head. And at last she decided that she would try it.

The woman took all the manioc pulp out of the tipity. Gently she placed her child so that he stood upright in the long tube of loosely woven vines. Little by little, she pulled its meshes tight until they were squeezing Pahy Tuna, as they squeezed the manioc.

And when she took the boy out again, her heart leaped for joy. The bumps were gone from his skin. He stood up straight and strong. His face and his form were handsomer than any child in the tribe. And she gave thanks to the Spirit of Moon Mirror Lake, who surely had had something to do with the miracle.

All went well until the other women noticed how often Ica went into the forest. They questioned her closely, and she guessed they suspected her unlawful secret.

"I shall put you in the keeping of the Spirit of our Lake," Ica told her son, who was by now able to walk and to talk and to understand why this must be. "She will turn you into a fine fish,

105

and you shall live with her in her lake-bottom home. Now and then I will come to visit you on the edge of the water. Then you shall change yourself back into a boy."

So it was that Pahy Tuna grew up safely in the land of the Woman Tribe. It was when he was almost grown that his mother's neighbors at last learned the secret of her visits to the lakeshore.

One day they watched her as she stood calling, "Pahy Tuna! Pahy Tuna!" And they saw a big fish swim out of the water and turn into a handsome young man.

One there was in that country who was determined to capture the youth. Some say it was a spiteful neighbor, jealous because she did not have such a son. They tell how she threw a net into the lake and caught the swimming fish. But the net was weak. And the fish was strong. Easily, Pahy Tuna broke through the net and swam safely away. A second and stronger net was broken the same way. But then the spiteful neighbor begged long strands of hair from the heads of the Amazons. With these she made a third net, a net which was so strong that no fish could break it, not even Pahy Tuna. He was caught at last.

What became of Pahy Tuna? No doubt his mother was punished by the other Warrior Women. No doubt Pahy Tuna, in his own form, was sent away when the men came for their next visit.

Was this story true? Who knows? However it was, the Spanish explorers named Brazil's mightiest stream, "River of the Amazons." So it is called today. And the little, green, lucky Amazon stones are still found, now and then, in ancient Indian huts that are hidden in the deep forests along its banks.

THE BEETLE AND THE PACA

A GREEN AND GOLD BEETLE was crawling, one day, on a leaf of a tree on the bank of the Amazon River. In the sun his back seemed dusted with gold. He was like a green and gold jewel, as bright as an emerald from the mines of this land of Brazil.

This emerald-green beetle lived in a forest which belonged to insects like him. That damp jungle belonged, too, to the butterflies and the birds, to the four-legged beasts, to the creatures that crawl and to the creatures that swim. It belonged to all these, but it did not really belong to man.

There were, of course, a few men in that land. On this day, there were the Indian boy, Manoel, and his old grandfather. But their small dugout canoe was the only boat on that part of the mighty stream.

It was bad luck for the emerald-green beetle that their canoe came so close to the riverbank. It was bad luck that the beetle's leaf hung so far out over the water. It was bad luck, too, that the sun made the beetle's back shine so brightly. For Manoel's sharp eyes caught its golden-green brightness, even on the green leaf.

"Paddle closer to land, Grandfather," the Indian boy said.

108

"Here's another green beetle. Soon I shall have enough of them to sell."

It may seem strange that a boy could get pesos for small beetles like these. But the Brazilian beetles were like jewels. Like jewels, they were often made into ornaments for people to wear.

"Do you know, Manoel, how that beetle got its emerald-green coat? Do you know why there is golden dust on its back?"

The old Indian grandfather laid down his paddle while the boy scooped the beetle into a small basket. It was good to rest under the trees there for a few moments. In their shade it was cooler than in the hot Brazilian sun, out on the river.

Manoel smiled. He liked to hear his grandfather tell tales of long ago magic. And on this day he listened happily to the story of how the Brazilian beetle got its green and gold coat.

In other times beetles were mostly of a brown color or dull black. It was a brown beetle about which the boy's grandfather was telling.

One day, this brown beetle was crawling slowly along a path on the riverbank. Little by little he made his way along under the trees.

"Good day, Beetle," a voice said over his head. It came from a green parrot with a bright golden head, perched on a low branch.

"Good day, Parrot," the brown beetle replied. The beetle could talk as well as the parrot. In those times, so long ago, all living things knew how to speak with one another.

Just then there came, running out of the bushes, a furry, brown and white paca. Pacas run fast. A hunter has to be quick to catch one of these rabbitlike rats for his cooking pot. This paca was

almost in the water before he could stop himself.

The parrot and the beetle laughed as the paca panted to get his breath. The paca laughed himself, and he called out, "Good day, Parrot! Good day, Beetle! What are you two doing on this fine morning?"

"Just resting," said the parrot.

"I'm going on a journey," the beetle said, starting to crawl away.

"A journey! Ha! Ha!" the paca laughed rudely. "Listen to that, Parrot! This brown beetle goes on a journey. He creeps so slowly, he hardly seems to be moving. Why don't you go faster, Beetle? Watch me, how I run! This is the speed you will need for a real journey."

The boastful paca ran quickly along the riverbank. And when he turned back, he kept on teasing the poor little brown beetle.

The green and yellow parrot looked on. He cocked his golden head as he listened. Then he blinked his small eyes, and he said, "You talk very big, Paca. Why don't you and our friend, Beetle, have a race? Sometimes the one who runs fastest does not win the race. You two shall go, each as fast as he can, to that big tree at the next bend in the river. The one who gets there first shall have a pretty new coat."

"A race!" The proud paca was delighted. "That will be easy for me to win." He was sure, much too sure, that the pretty new coat would be his.

"A soft yellow coat with fine black spots! That is what I would choose. A coat like a jaguar's! And I want a tail, too, long like a jaguar's tail."

The paca admired the big spotted cat above all other beasts.

111

The jaguar was so big and so strong. And he had such a splendid tail. The poor paca, as everyone knows, had almost no tail at all.

"I shall do my best," the brown beetle said in his turn. A happy thought had just come to him as he looked up at the parrot, stretching his green wings in the sunshine.

"And if I should win this race, Parrot," the beetle continued, "I should like a new coat the color of your green wings. It should be dusted with gold, yellow like your own head."

Well, the strange race began.

"Go!" cried the parrot. And he himself flew off ahead to the tree at the river's bend. Sitting there on a low branch he waited for his two friends.

"I'm off! Good-bye, Beetle!" the paca called back over his shoulder. He took several running steps. Then he slowed down.

"Why should I hurry? A race with a slowpoke of a beetle, for me, is only a joke."

So the paca stopped for a little drink at the river's edge. Then he just trotted along at a comfortable pace.

But when the paca came to the big tree at the bend in the river, the little brown beetle was already there.

"Wherever have you been, Paca?" the beetle called out from the trunk of the tree. "What a slowpoke you are? Why were you so long?" Now it was the beetle's turn to tease.

The paca did not know what to reply. His eyes were round with his surprise. His little chin dropped. He looked so funny that the parrot opened his gray beak and laughed and laughed.

"How ever did you get here before me, Beetle?" cried the paca. "How could you run so much faster than I?"

"Oh, I did not run, Paca."

112

"Well, surely you could not crawl so fast?"

"No, I did not crawl." The beetle was laughing, too.

"Did you swim, Beetle? How could you swim as quickly as I could run?"

"I did not swim either," the beetle replied. "Yet, I got here first. The parrot can tell you that."

"Well, then, how ever *did* you get here? It must be some trick."

"No trick at all," the beetle said. "I flew."

"Have you forgotten, my proud Paca, that beetles can fly?" The parrot put his word into the discussion. "I did not say that, in this race, either one of you must run, or crawl, or swim. I said you must 'go.' "

"The parrot said only, 'Go as fast as you can!' " The beetle was triumphant. "I reached this tree first. I get the pretty new coat."

The paca hung his head. He had been just a little too proud of his swift running. He had, indeed, forgotten that a beetle can fly. Off he went into the bushes in his same old brown coat with its little white spots.

"Come back, Paca!" the beetle called after him. "Come back and see my shining green coat! Come back and admire its thousands of specks of gold!"

But the paca did not come back. To this day a paca's coat is dull brown. His spots are pale and small, not at all like a jaguar's. And his tiny tail is still almost no tail at all.

CHILDREN OF THE SUN

OF ALL THE INTERESTING Indian peoples of South America, perhaps the most interesting were the ancient Incas. They lived in the highlands of Peru in the shadow of the snow-peaked Andes Mountains. And even so long ago, they had temples and palaces whose like was not known anywhere else in the world.

"We are the children of Inti, the Sun-god himself," they declared. And their story is told in countless different legends.

In the beginning, they said, the Maker-of-All-Things, Pachacamac, gave his orders, "Let there be earth, and let there be sky! Let there be day, and let there be night! Let the sun and moon shine! Let a man be! And a woman, too!" And it was so.

Pachacamac shaped all the people of the world from soft lumps of clay. He painted their faces with the colors of the skins he wanted them to have. Those who were to wear their hair short, he painted with short hair. Those who were to let it grow long, he painted with long hair. Upon each one he painted a different dress.

The Creator-god put breath into the bodies of his clay figures. He gave them their souls, and he told them the words they should speak, the songs they should sing. He gave them the seeds they

115

should plant, and showed them the food they should eat.

At first men and women had plenty. Pacha-Mama, whom Pacha-camac named the Earth-Mother, helped them produce their grain and their fruits. No one was hungry.

But they soon forgot the wise words of Pachacamac who had told them what they must do for themselves. They became little better than the wild animals. They planted no seeds. They wove no cloth for making their ponchos. They took no thought of anything beyond fighting with one another and filling their stomachs with wild fruits and the beasts they could kill.

It was when the people lived like this, that the earth grew dark. The sky became so black that men were afraid. Then, from a cliff beside the lake called Titicaca, there was seen a bright light. It was so strong that one could not gaze long upon its golden glory. This was because it came from the very Sun-god himself, from Inti whom Pachacamac had sent to bring light again to the dark world.

Not long thereafter, two strange figures came to the high country. Dressed in ponchos of fine weave, a man and a woman walked there among the savage people. They were, so the legends say, Manco Capac and his sister-wife, Mama Oullo, the children of Inti. They had been sent by the Sun-god to teach men and women once again how they should live.

Good luck walked with Manco Capac and Mama Oullo because the man carried the golden staff of the Sun-god. That golden staff was strong, for all it was only as wide as his two fingers, and only as long as his arm.

"When we can drive Inti's golden staff into the ground with one single thrust, we shall have found the place for our temple," Manco Capac told Mama Oullo. Again and again he halted their pace.

Again and again he tried to drive the golden staff into the ground. But each time he found he could not sink even its point in the earth.

So they went on and on. And at last they came to a fair valley in the heart of those highlands. There a rainbow appeared, and the magic staff sank deep into the earth. Manco Capac rejoiced that his long journey was ended. He called all the people of that place together, and from a high rock he spoke to them.

"Know, good people," he cried, "that I am the first Inca to be called Manco Capac. I am the son of Inti, the Sun-god. And I am sent by him to rule over your land and to teach you once more how Pachacamac wants you to live."

"We do not bow to the Sun-god here, Stranger," the people made answer. "Our God is Pachacamac, the Maker-of-All-Things. Why should we bow to the sun who is so weak that he permits clouds to cover his face? Many things happen when Inti is out of our sight. Plants grow in the earth. Animals are born in the forests. Fish swim in the streams when the sun is away as well as when he looks down upon the earth from the sky.

"How can the sun be a god? He travels over the blue bowl of the heavens always on the same path. He is not a free creature, going here and there as he likes. He is more like a slave who is told just where he shall go, day after day."

"All that is true, my good people," Manco Capac replied. "Pachacamac, the All-Highest, indeed, made all things. He formed the world with his thunder. He raised up the mountains. He pressed down the valleys. He filled the lakes with clear water, and he put men and women upon the earth. He even made Inti, the Sun-god to bless you.

"But Pachacamac does not take care of you now. He has appointed Inti your loving father. Inti smiles upon you. He sends you light and warmth without which you could not live. He makes your seeds grow. He ripens your fruits. Each day he crosses the blue bowl of the sky to make sure all is well with you.

"Why should you make temples for Pachacamac when the world itself is his temple? Why should you lay before him the gifts which are of his own making. No, it is to Inti, the Sun-god, whom you should pray. It is Inti you should thank that we Incas have come to show you the good way of life."

The highland people were pleased with the things which Manco Capac and Mama Oullo taught them. The First Inca showed the men how to plant seeds which would bring them plenty of food. He helped them to cut little flat fields out of the hillsides, like so many steps. He showed them how to turn the mountain streams into these fields so that their plants always had enough water. There was corn to make bread enough for all.

Manco Capac also took the men to hunt the wild beasts of those highlands: the vicunas, the guanacos, the alpacas, and the llamas. Alpacas and llamas were tamed and gathered in herds upon the upland plains. There was meat, too, for all.

Mama Oullo and the women spun and wove the soft wool of these highland animals. They made fine cloth which they dyed with bright colors from plants. And from the hides of the beasts they learned to fashion leather sandals to spare their bare feet from the rocky soil.

Soon the tamed llamas were bearing the loads of those lucky people. Soon huts of stone sheltered them from the winds and the mountain chill. And for holding their food and their drinks, they

118

baked bowls which they had shaped out of clay.

A great city rose on the spot where Manco Capac's golden staff sank into the ground. The Incas called their city Cuzco, which is to say, "Heart of the World." Even today its ruins tell of its splendor.

The Inca city had temples and houses covered with shining gold; golden gardens, with soil of fine golden powder; golden cornstalks, with long, round golden ears; golden pots in which there were bright golden flowers; birds, butterflies, and bees; rabbits and lizards of gold, all made by the Inca goldsmiths, were there among the gold bushes. Even a flock of gold sheep and lambs were to be seen, tended by shepherd figures with crooks of pure gold.

Oh, there was gold in plenty in the land of the Incas. There was gold in the mountain streams, and gold and silver, too, under the ground. Inside the palaces of these Children-of-the-Sun, curious objects were molded and carved from these precious metals. Kitchen pots and pans, logs for the hearth, baskets and ropes, shovels and spades, indeed, all the things which were then used by the Incas, had their doubles in metal.

It was the Inca custom to wear ornaments in their ears. Through the holes which were pierced through them, they put pins of gold. These pins were made thicker and thicker until they were plugs which stretched the holes until they would hold wheels of gold a full three inches across. It was because of this strange fashion, that the first Spanish travelers gave the Incas the nickname, "Big Ears."

For building the houses and temples of their Inca rulers, the Indians of the Andes were made to lay up walls of brick and stone. These were fitted together so tightly that not even a needle could be pushed in between them. The Indians also built for their masters long bathing pools, lined with smooth stone, into which were brought streams of water, both hot and cold.

Outside of Cuzco, too, there were Inca wonders to tell of. Roads paved with smooth stone led out from the city in all four directions.

"As the rays of Inti, our Sun-Father, find their way to all parts of the earth, so shall our kingdom reach out to the north and the south, the east and the west." This was the Inca boast.

One by one, the powerful Incas gathered the Indian tribes under their rule. More and more came with offerings to the Sun-god. In greater numbers they bowed before Inti's great altar with its huge golden sun disk. This was studded with gems so bright that it was said a man would go blind if he gazed upon it too long.

Thousands of young shepherds tended the llamas of the Inca kings. Thousands more hunted the wild vicunas to get their soft wool for making the royal robes. A thousand beautiful Indian girls, the "Maids-of-the-Sun," lived in a magnificent palace. There they spent their days spinning and weaving, dyeing and embroidering the Incas' splendid garments.

Sometimes the Sun-Maids wove into their cloth threads of pure gold. Sometimes they sewed upon the robes they made tiny leaves of bright silver, or bits of mother-of-pearl. Instead of fringe on their edges, they often finished these garments with rows of bright-colored feathers.

In those times, everything belonged to the Inca kings. The flocks and the fields. The gold mines and the silver mines. Even the wild beasts on the mountains and the fish in the streams.

Sometimes, the Indians grumbled to themselves. "How do we know that these men who rule us, are truly Children-of-the-Sun?"

One of these was a young shepherd. As he led his flocks to the drinking fountain, he saw that the sun shone on the water. Its rays fell on a bit of clear crystal that lay on the bottom of the shallow drinking pool. As the young shepherd looked down, as if in a mirror, he saw, looking over his shoulder, the bright image of Inti, the very Sun-god himself.

"He! Eh! my friends," he said as he ran to his fellow herdsmen, "I have seen the Sun-god, and he looks just like the great Inca. He wears the same royal fringe of black hair on his forehead. He has the same golden wheels in his ears. Golden rays light his head. It surely was the Sun-god, the great Inti, himself that I saw in the pool."

After that, so they say, the Indians of those Peruvian highlands were sure that the Incas were, indeed, Children-of-the-Sun.

This whole story has really been given over to describe the Incas and the way people today think that they lived. How much of it is true, who can say? Most of its facts have been gathered by men who have explored the Cuzco ruins of later times and who have studied the ancient writings of those who lived in Peru long, long ago. It has been put into this book because there will follow some fairy tales about happenings in Inca times.

GOLDEN FLOWER AND THE
THREE WARRIORS

THE ANDES MOUNTAINS of Peru are among the wonders of the world. Their snow-capped pointed peaks seem to pierce the sky. Their giant rocks have such curious forms that surely Pachacamac must have laughed when he gave them their shapes.

Rocks just like the wishbone of a chicken. Rocks that stand like the walls of a temple. Rocks arranged like a church. One as big as a rancho and shaped like a turtle. People called that one The Tortoise. And there was another which they named the Rock King because it looked like a man sitting high on a throne. Also, in one place there were rock pillars spread over the land like a forest of trees.

It is not strange that the people said Pachacamac had molded these high mountains and curious rocks. No wonder either that they told so many stories about them.

There was, for example, the tale about the Three Mountains that lie near the town which men call Huanuco. This was the story about the girl, Golden Flower, and the Three Warriors. It was Golden Flower, the chief's daughter, who drew the three thither. And it was those three warriors who were turned into the three mountain peaks.

It happened in Inca times, long, long ago, when men still prayed to Pachacamac and worshipped Inti, the Sun-god.

123

In one part of Peru, there was a certain Inca tribe called the Pillco. And since its chief was named Rumi, he was known far and wide as Pillco-Rumi. This man was the ruler of his part of the country, but of course the land really belonged to the Great Inca. Everyone in it had to live by his laws.

Being a chief, Pillco-Rumi had many wives. Though he had always longed for a daughter, all his children were boys. It was not until he had already had fifty sons, that a girl-child was born to him.

Pillco-Rumi loved this daughter. She was dearest to him among all his children. So fair was she that when she walked abroad with her maidens, people stared at her, speechless. Like the sun, her beauty almost blinded them. She was well-called, they thought, Cori-Huayti, or Golden Flower.

When she was of an age to be married, the fame of Golden Flower's loveliness had spread through her land and into far countries too. All the young men waited with eager hearts to learn whom she would marry when she was eighteen. It was the law of the Incas, then, that at the Spring Festival each year, the young men who had reached the age of twenty years must take a wife. All the girls of eighteen must accept a husband.

This law brought sadness to the heart of the Chief, Pillco-Rumi. He could not bear the thought of giving up his dear daughter.

"My Golden Flower is too fair and too fine to wed any man," the Chief said to his counselors. "She is a bride fit for the Sun-god himself. I shall give her up to no other bridegroom."

"But the law of the Great Inca may not be put aside," the wise counselors reminded their Chief. "If she will not wed, there is only one road which your daughter may travel. And that leads to prison

124

through the gate of the Temple of the Maids-of-the-Sun."

The Chief shook his head stubbornly. "In the temple of the Sun-Maids, Golden Flower would be lost to me. And she would be only one among a thousand others who serve the sun there. Better, far better, that Inti, the Sun-god, should take her himself to his kingdom up in the sky."

Well, one day, just before the Spring Festival, there knocked at Pillco-Rumi's gate three messengers from afar. One came from Runtus, a famous warrior who lived in a land by the sea. Men also called this Runtus, The White-Haired-One, for he was old and his hair was no longer black.

The second messenger had been sent by the strong, mighty warrior, Maray, whose tribe roamed the high plains and whose nickname was Man-of-Stone.

The third brought word from Paucar of the forest tribes. Paucar was a warrior so young and so handsome that, wherever he went, young girls threw flower wreaths over his head.

In their own parts of the country, these three warriors had heard of the beauty of Golden Flower, the Pillco Chief's daughter. They knew that, like all the other maids of eighteen in Inca lands, she must shortly be wed.

"My master, Runtus, will come at the head of his army to take Golden Flower for his wife," said the first messenger. "Runtus is old. That is true. But with age goes wisdom. He will know well how to make a wife happy."

"My master, Maray, also wishes to wed Golden Flower," the second messenger cried. "He, too, will come with his army on the day of the Spring Festival. Not for nothing is Maray known as Man-of-Stone. Maray is strong. The maid is weak. And the weak

125

need the strong. Your daughter will be protected from all harm when she is wed to Maray, O Chief."

Then the third messenger spoke.

"My master, young Paucar, means to take Golden Flower for his bride at the Spring Festival. He brings a great army of young heroes like himself so that no one shall prevent his wedding the Chief's daughter. Old White-Hair may be wise. Man-of-Stone may be strong. But Paucar is young and Paucar is handsome. He knows how to soften the heart of a girl. Golden Flower will surely prefer him to all others as a husband."

But the Chief of the Pillco Tribe sent these messengers home without any answers. Because of the Great Inca's law, he was afraid to say he would not permit his daughter to marry. Yet he still was determined that he would give her up only when she became the bride of the Sun-god himself.

The day of the Spring Festival dawned. The people were gathered in the open square of the town. Girls were dressed for their weddings. Youths were clad in their best. There was music and singing, and all were rejoicing that, this year, their Chief's daughter would take part in the ceremonies.

Golden Flower, however, was not in the square to join in the merrymaking. She was waiting for her father in her garden, and she knew nothing of his decision that she should not be given in marriage. Like all the other girls of her age, she was wondering what kind of a husband the day would bring to her.

Meanwhile, her father, the Chief Pillco-Rumi, had climbed up into the lookout tower facing the west. From that high place, he could see far, far over the land. And as his eyes searched the horizon, where the sky meets the earth, he saw three clouds of dust.

126

"The three warriors are coming," he cried. "From the forest, the plains, and the land by the sea they come. And they bring their armies with them. Nothing can save my dear daughter now but Inti, the Sun-god."

Pillco-Rumi lifted his face to the heavens. He stretched his arms upward. "Oh, Sun-god," he prayed, "oh, Inti, thou who art son to Pachacamac, the Maker-of-All-Things. To none but thee will I give up my dear Golden Flower. Descend and take her for thy bride."

Then the Chief made his way down out of the tower, for the people were calling for him. Word had spread through the crowd that the warriors were coming and that their armies were near. There would be a terrible battle.

"Save us, Pillco-Rumi! Save us from these armies," they begged of their Chief, who now stood with his daughter in the open square.

"I have prayed to the Sun-god," he told them. "You must pray to him also. Only the Sun-god can save us from the three warriors."

"The Sun-god! The Sun-god! Protect us, O Sun-god!" These cries rang through the square.

Inti must have heard them. He must have looked down with pity upon the father's distress. The watchers in the towers of his temple saw with their own eyes the wonders he wrought.

A dazzling rainbow appeared in the blue bowl of the sky. And standing high on its arch, as if on a bridge, was the Sun-god himself. No doubt his father, Pachacamac, the All-Powerful, was behind him, ready to lend his mighty aid. For this is what happened.

Paucar was the swiftest of the three warriors. With his army of heroes, the handsome, young suitor had come nearest the city. At the very place where he marched, there rose a high mountain whose peak was covered with snow. That snow melted quickly

127

under the fierce rays of the sun. It flowed down the steep side of the mountain to form a broad river with deep rushing waters.

Other mountains were thrown up out of the earth where the two warriors, Maray and Old Runtus, stood. With his magic might, the Sun-god turned all three warriors and their armies into stone. And that was the last that ever was seen of these eager suitors of Cori-Huayti, Golden Flower.

Three rocky mountains bear the names of the would-be husbands of the Pillco Chief's daughter. Mt. Rondos is Runtus. Children who live in its shadow like to think they see in the mountain's shape, an old man lying asleep on his back, with his arms crossed on his breast.

Mt. Maramba, whose name surely comes from Maray, looks like a man sitting down, like the Man-of-Stone resting after his labors.

Mt. Paucarbamba, the third mountain, is shaped like a young warrior, standing up straight and fierce, with his head in the sky.

From his place on the rainbow bridge, the Sun-god looked down upon the fair daughter of Pillco-Rumi. Like thunder, his voice rang across the bright heavens and over the earth.

"*Huanucuy!*" he called. All the people there heard him. They held their breath, for they knew that the word meant "Live no more on earth!"

As they watched, they saw Inti, the Sun-god, reach down and take the hand of Golden Flower. They marveled as he led the girl across his curved rainbow bridge to dwell with him as his bride in his palace in the sky.

It is the word which Inti spoke that day which gave those people the name for the new city they built. They called it Huanuco which surely was the very same as the Sun-god's cry, "Huanucuy."

128

THE MAGIC PONCHO

ALLPA WAS A YOUNG herdsman who lived in the ancient times of the Incas. He dwelt with his old mother in a little stone hut outside the great city of Cuzco in the Peruvian highlands. A fine lad he was, gentle and kind, which is why he was known as Allpa or "Good One."

Each day this young herdsman wandered over the meadows which belonged to the Great Inca. From sunrise to sunset, he watched over the royal llamas and alpacas while they grazed under the blue sky. From the meadows, the youth could see the splendid palaces of his royal master. Sometimes he talked with the other shepherds about the fine palace folk. Sometimes, in whispers, they spoke of the Sun Princesses, the young girls who lived in the house of Inti, the Sun-god.

"The Maids-of-the-Sun are as fair as the moon," the young men sighed. "But alas, like the moon, they are wed to the sun. They are not for ordinary men like us."

It was because this was true that the beautiful brides of Inti were kept shut up behind the stone walls of their palace. When they set foot outside its carved gates, guards watched them until

129

they came back in again. Common folk, like these shepherds, dared not lift their eyes to them.

Now, among the thousand beautiful Sun Princesses there was one far lovelier than all the rest. She was as slender and graceful as the dancing shadow of a shepherd's staff. She was as sweet as a spring morning. And her name was Sapa Ñusta, or Princess Most Fair.

The lovely Sapa Ñusta always worked well at her spinning. She sang at her weaving, and she knew how to make the good drink, chicha, as the Inca liked it best. But sometimes she grew tired of the high walls of the Sun Palace.

"Let us walk out into the world and see something new," she would say to her palace companions. And she would smile sweetly at the friendly gate guard and promise him that they would not go out of his sight.

One day while Sapa Ñusta and three of her friends strolled over the meadows, they came upon Allpa, the young shepherd, tending his flocks. Clear, sweet notes flowed from the flute which he held to his lips as he lolled on a low rock in the warm sunshine. The four princesses stopped to listen and to play with the tame llamas.

"These llamas of the Great Inca are such pretty white llamas. I never have seen prettier, Shepherd," Sapa Ñusta cried out in her delight.

The shepherd opened his lips to answer, but no words came. He was struck dumb with wonder and awe at the beauty of the four Sun Princesses. It was as if the four figures in the fountains which flowed out to the four ends of the Inca's kingdom had come to life, before his eyes. As he stared at them, the good youth was dazzled, above all, by the loveliness of the fair Sapa Ñusta.

131

For their part, the four princesses were well pleased with the young herdsman. Allpa stood straight and strong. He made a fine figure, with his shepherd's crook in his hand, with his eyes so steady and clear. His head was set nobly upon his broad shoulders, and a silver ornament hung proudly upon his smooth brow.

"Why do you not answer us, Shepherd?" Sapa Ñusta asked, looking over her shoulder to make sure the guard was not watching too closely.

"Have no fear to speak to us because we are Sun-Maids. The gate guard is our friend. No harm shall come to you."

Then Allpa fell to his knees. He kissed the edge of her soft woolen gown. "Not often, Princess, does the bright Moon-goddess walk on the earth. It is not strange that a poor shepherd like me should be awed by your shining beauty."

The princesses put the young man at his ease. They examined the square silver plate he wore on his forehead and admired the man and the girl and the round heart carved upon it. They asked him to play on his flute, and all through the afternoon Allpa made for them his sweet shepherd's music.

When the sun was low in the sky, the handsome young herdsman led his llamas away to their corral for the night. The Sun Princesses made their way back to their palace. At its gate they stopped to let the guard know that their day in the meadows had done them much good.

That evening Sapa Ñusta could not eat her supper. Nor could she sleep when she lay herself down on her couch. Even when she shut her eyes, she could not drive away the image of the young herdsman with the silver square on his brow. The birds had already begun to sing of the dawn before she dropped off to sleep.

132

Many such afternoons after that this Princess-Most-Fair spent out on the meadows with Allpa, the shepherd. Each evening she came back to the palace, both happy and sad. For she knew now that she loved the youth. And she knew Allpa loved her. But she knew, too, that as a Sun Princess, she had sworn to be true to Inti. No man could she ever wed, least of all a poor shepherd.

One night, when sleep came to her, Sapa Ñusta had a strange dream. She thought that a singing bird lit on her shoulder.

"Why are you sad, Ñusta?" She dreamed the bird spoke these words.

"Ah, my flying friend, I am in love with Allpa, the shepherd youth. And it means death for us both, if our love is found out."

"Go for help, Sun-Maid, to the four fountains that flow toward the four corners of the kingdom. Sit there between them. Sing them your heart's desire. If the waters give back your song, all will be well. If they are silent, truly bad luck will come to you."

Next morning, with her dream still clear in her mind, the Princess-Most-Fair went to the four fountains. Sitting beside them, she sang her song thus:

> *Upon a shepherd's brow is laid,*
> *A silver square, with man and maid*
> *And loving heart in its design.*

> *"Oh Fountain, make their story mine!"*

Then she held her breath. She was almost afraid to listen, lest she hear no reply. But, one by one, the four fountains took up her song. One by one, their falling waters sang her song back to her. When she went once more to her room in the palace, there was hope in her heart.

133

Meanwhile, out on the meadow in the hut of the young shepherd, all was sorrow and gloom. Allpa also knew it was death for a herdsman to love a Princess-of-the-Sun. The young man played on his flute tunes so sad that even the llamas drooped their proud heads. He wept bitter tears. He did not eat. He did not sleep. So deeply he grieved that he became ill, and his mother feared for his life. She gathered fine herbs, and she made him a strong broth.

"Drink this, my son," she said. "A broth of good herbs will cure anything, even a lover's grief." But although Allpa drank the hot broth, no hope lightened his heart. He was as ill as before.

"Lie here by the fire, my son. I will cover you with the white poncho which your grandmother left for you. She declared it had once belonged to Pachacamac himself. He is the Life-Giver, and may this poncho give life to you."

The woman spread over him the poncho made of the wool of a pure white llama. In those olden times, such a garment was worn only by an Inca, a Child-of-the-Sun.

As soon as she could, Sapa Ñusta set out with her companions to look for her shepherd. She wanted to tell him of her strange dream and how the four fountains gave back her song to her. When she could not find him out with the llamas and the alpacas, she made her way to his hut.

"Good day, Mamita," she spoke politely to the woman who answered her knock. "We are tired and thirsty. We pray you, give us a drink."

The woman looked toward the corner where her son lay covered with the white poncho. He had pulled it up over his head, and he lay very still, as though he was asleep.

"What do you seek here, Princess?" the woman asked as she

handed the drinking bowl to the girl. She knew from their fine clothes that these girls came from Inti's palace. And by the things her son had told her, she guessed that this one was the Sun-Maid he loved.

"I seek Allpa, the shepherd. I have a message for him that will bring him joy." The girl's eyes were happy and eager when the woman lifted up the white poncho. Then her face fell, and she stared at the corner of the room with surprise. For where Allpa had been lying, there was now no one, no one at all.

The shepherd youth's mother screamed.

"He was there. Now he is gone. Alas, my son has gone from me. It is you, Princess, who have brought this sadness to my house. Go away, Sapa Ñusta! Go away! You have taken my son. You may as well take his poncho, too. I never wish to see it again." And the weeping woman thrust the white poncho into the girl's hands.

Try as she would, the poor princess could not comfort the mother of the young herdsman. There was nothing for her to do but to throw the poncho over her shoulder and go back to the palace.

The guard at the gate saw the white poncho. But it seemed like any other, so no questions were asked. She went early to her own little room in the palace so that she might be by herself. So weary was she, and so worn with weeping, that she soon fell asleep.

Then a voice woke her, whispering, "Ñusta! Sapa Ñusta!" She started up from her couch. She could not believe her own ears. Nor could she believe her eyes. For she thought she saw sitting on the foot of her couch, her beloved Allpa, the herdsman.

"*Sh!* my Ñusta," he whispered. "Do not fear. The magic poncho of Pachacamac has brought me safely into your palace. It will take me safely out again in the same way. When morning comes, we

135

shall go far, far away, where they cannot find us. Like the man and the maid on my headplate, we shall be happy together."

It happened just so. Next morning as if nothing strange had occurred, the Princess-Most-Fair walked out through the palace gate. The white poncho lay carelessly thrown over her shoulder as on the evening before. But this time, there was no other Maid-of-the-Sun with her. The guard was surprised that she should be allowed to go out on the meadows alone. He followed her at a distance. And when she spread out the poncho, he saw the young herdsman rise from its folds. Frightened at this strange sight, he gave the alarm.

Perhaps the white poncho still made its magic. Perhaps it hid the two young lovers from the sight of their pursuers. The guards ran as fast as ever they could. But they could not seem to catch up with the two, the shepherd and the Sun-Maid.

Over the meadows and up the steep mountainsides, they fled like two wild vicunas. Perhaps they found up there a safe hiding place behind the rocks. Perhaps they went on to another land out of the reach of the Inca guards.

Some people think that a curious rock high up the mountain is Sapa Ñusta, the Princess-Most-Fair. They say Inti turned her into stone when his guards could not bring her back to him. They point out a tall, slim rock which looks like a girl. One arm is raised high, and in her hand there is a stone that looks like a shoe, ready to be thrown at any one who may try to take her away from her shepherd.

136

MARIO AND THE YARA

IF THERE WERE GODS in the sky, and spirits in the trees, why should there not also have been nymphs in the rivers and lakes?

In ancient times, many a young man said he had seen such a water-spirit. There was even a name for her. They called her a Yara.

A Yara had a head, shoulders, and body like those of any girl that lived on the land. But instead of two legs, she had a long shining tail like that of a fish.

A Yara had magic beauty. Seen in the half light of the evening, or in the faint glow of the rising moon, she was often enchanting.

That was the trouble. Once a young man fell under the spell of a Yara, he was lost to this world. Take Mario for example.

Mario was a fine young fellow, and well loved in his village. He was good with the fishing spear and with the bow and arrows also. Everyone thought that his sweetheart, Camila, had made a wise choice when she promised to marry him.

Only his old grandmother shook her head when Mario set forth to hunt or to fish when the day was nearing its end.

"Take care, Mario," she said again and again. "You are soon to

marry Camila. It is because of just that that it is dangerous for you to walk on the riverbanks at this time of day. Take care, my son, that you do not meet a Yara who will lead you clear out of this world.

"It is young men like you, those just ready to take a bride, to whom the water-nymph appears. It may be she is jealous of your earthly sweetheart. It may be she wants you for her own husband. I beg you, do your hunting and fishing when the day is bright and the sun is high."

But, like many young people in many lands, Mario paid little attention to the warnings of his wise grandmother. He did not believe in her tales of water-nymphs who led young men so far into the deep forest that they could never come back. He went his way as he always had. If the fish were swimming near the land, or if the hunting was unusually good, he stayed out on the riverbank until the night fell. He did not come home until it was too dark for him to aim his sharp arrows.

Late one such evening, Mario walked slowly along the bank of a dark stream. The trees met over his head in a green arch that almost shut out the daylight. The sun had set. A pale round moon hung in the sky.

Suddenly the young man heard the sound of sweet singing. It seemed to come from far up the river, and Mario followed the sound. In the faint light of the moon, he spied a figure in white, sitting high on a rock that rose out of the water. Softly, softly, Mario crept nearer to find out who it could be. From the bank he could see it was a beautiful girl, bathed in white light.

"So lovely a sight, I never have seen!" the young man said to himself. He stood speechless with delight, watching the girl twine

139

sweet-smelling white blossoms into her long black hair. Her song was soft and low, and a little sad, too. And it twisted the very heart of the listening Mario. Not until the song ceased was the spell lifted. Not until then could he stir from the spot where he stood.

Mario moved nearer. He wanted to see the girl's face more clearly. He did not believe that she could be as beautiful as she looked there in the pale light of the moon.

But before he could reach the rock, the white figure dived into the river. Mario thought he heard her laugh, teasing him, as she swam swiftly away.

That night when he paid a visit to his sweetheart, Camila, Mario told her of the girl on the rock, and the songs she had sung.

"Who could she be, Camila?" he asked. "I never have seen her here in our village. I never have heard such sweet singing as hers."

The girl, Camila, burst into tears. She trembled like a leaf in the wind.

"Alas, Mario," she cried. "That was no earthly girl. That was a Yara. I know it as well as if I had seen her myself. Trouble is sure to come to us now. Oh, my Mario, do not go to that river again. Give me your promise that you will hunt only in the deep woods far from the stream! Say you will not try to find the girl on the rock again!"

Mario promised. For several days he kept away from the stream where he had seen the water-nymph. But he could not put the thought of her out of his mind. Her songs rang in his ears.

How beautiful she had been, sitting in the moonlight on the dark rock! No bird ever had sung more sweetly. It seemed to the young hunter that he must see her just once again. What harm could it do? He could still marry Camila. So much did he think

140

about the enchanting Yara, that he forgot all about the promise which he had made to his weeping sweetheart.

He had no trouble in finding the Yara, no trouble at all. She sat, as before, upon the dark rock in the river, twining a garland of white flowers in her black hair.

She shines like the moon, the young man thought, as its light fell on her face.

Again her sweet singing filled the dark forest. And again the water-nymph dived into the river when Mario approached. This time instead of laughing to tease him, she smiled at him sweetly. With one pale hand she beckoned to him to follow her.

Then, Mario was frightened. Could his grandmother and his bride to be have spoken truly? Could so lovely a girl as this, indeed, be a Yara?

He remembered strange things that had happened to his friends, who, like himself, were about to be married. There was Luis, who had failed to come home from fishing in this very river. His spear and his arrows, also the fish he had caught, were found on the bank. But no one had ever seen him again. Then there was José. What had become of him on the evening he went out alone to hunt?

Mario ran away as fast as he could. He did not look back when the sound of the girl's singing floated to his ears out of the darkness.

But that night, in his hammock, he could not sleep. Had it perhaps been a dream? Had he really seen anything but a patch of moonlight on a rock? Had he imagined the sweet songs in the evening stillness?

These questions plagued him. He could not stop wondering. And the next day, at dusk, he went for a third time to the Yara's stream.

141

Now the moonlight seemed brighter. It played on the black waters and made a bright silver path. In the center of the path, the waters seemed to part, and the nymph appeared. She was more lovely than ever, so poor Mario thought. His heart beat faster and faster as he gazed on her pale face and listened to her sweet voice. He stood as if turned to stone. He was as much her prisoner as if he had been lashed to a tree.

Then, it was as if Camila spoke to him. As clear as a night-bird's call, her voice was in his ears, crying. "God protect you, my Mario! Take care! Oh, take care!"

This seemed to bring the young man to his senses. He raised his bow and aimed at the heart of the Yara. His arrow sped straight and true. And the water-nymph was no longer there.

At first Mario thought that his arrow had found her heart. But then there came the sound of her mocking laughter, tinkling like falling water. This time she was closer to the young hunter, standing straight up in the parting of the rippling waters.

A second time, a third time, even a fourth time, Mario shot an arrow towards the nymph's white figure. But each fell harmlessly into the moonlit stream. Each time the Yara only drew nearer to him.

"Why do you fear me so, good Mario?" the Yara asked softly. She was now so close to the bank that the young man could look into her green eyes. He could smell the white flowers which she wore as a wreath on her head, and he thought they were like the stars in the night sky. Then the Yara began to sing softly again. Slowly she moved off up the river, beckoning gently.

Gone was all thought of his sweetheart Camila. No word of his grandmother's warning did Mario remember now. The spell of the

142

water-nymph was full upon him. Step by step he followed her. On, on, and on she led him farther from his home.

Never did his grandmother or his Camila see Mario again. The people then said that those who enter the watery realm of the Yaras do not come back again.

THE GIANT SNAKE THAT
SWALLOWED A GIRL

IT HAPPENED ONE TIME that a certain Indian named Magu spent the night far out in the jungle of the South American land known as Colombia. He made himself a soft bed of leaves on the bank of a stream, and he slept soundly.

When he awoke in the morning, he felt something move close to his side. And to his horror he saw that he had for a bedfellow an enormous snake. It was an anaconda, the largest snake to be found anywhere in the jungle. Magu could see its spots clearly as it crawled away and slipped into the river.

"I have had a narrow escape," Magu said to himself. "For while the anaconda does not bite, its strong coils could easily have crushed me while I slept."

Magu stood up on his feet, and he looked all around to make sure that no other serpent was near. It was then he discovered that the giant snake that had shared his bed had left an egg in the leaves. It was a soft, leathery egg, and almost as big as a gourd.

"Ho, this will amuse my wife and my little girl Mina." Magu picked up the great egg and carried it home.

There he told his strange tale. When his wife and his child had

144

examined the egg, they laid it on a warm ledge near the cooking fire. They forgot it until fourteen days had gone by. Then the egg's covering broke, and a young anaconda crawled out.

"Kill the snake! Kill it, my husband!" Magu's wife cried. Her little girl Mina ran to the other side of the hut.

"But, no," said Magu. "Why should we kill such a pretty young creature? See its handsome markings! Look how big it is! An anaconda has no teeth and no poison. I shall keep it for a pet."

"Ah, but an anaconda can squeeze, Magu," the man's wife still objected. "An anaconda can swallow a pig or a goat. I do not like having a giant snake live in our hut."

"Now, Wife," said the Indian, "I will give my snake animals out of my traps in the jungle. I will feed it fish from the river. It shall have its stomach well filled at all times. Then it will be content. It will harm no one."

It was curious that the anaconda so quickly was tamed. It lived happily inside the Indian's hut. The man brought it plenty of small animals and fish, which it greatly liked. When Magu called "Boya! Boya!" the snake would crawl out of its corner and swallow its meal with one mighty gulp. It ate and it ate. It grew and it grew. It was truly much bigger than any other anaconda in the jungle.

Magu's pet snake was so long it would reach from the ridge of his roof to the ground. Its body was thicker than a man's thigh. And it was tame, just as tame as Mina's pet parrot, which would sit on her shoulder and pretend to nibble her ear.

The snake seemed to love its Indian master. Sometimes it followed him into the forest and looped itself on a tree branch nearby while the man fished or shot turtles with his flying arrows. Always it came back with him to the hut when the night fell.

145

Magu's wife and daughter did not like the serpent so well. The woman shook her head and said over and over, "This is not good, my husband. One day you will be sorry." And Mina was always a little afraid of the giant snake.

Now Magu loved his small daughter Mina almost more than anything else in the world. It was of her that the tame anaconda seemed to be jealous. Whenever the man played with Mina or petted her, the brown snake would coil itself sulkily up in a corner. It would not come out again until Magu had called it and called it. Yet his wife had to admit that the strange pet had never tried to do the child harm.

One day a fine feast was to be held in a neighboring village. For weeks the family in Magu's little hut had been talking of the eating and drinking, the singing and dancing that there would be.

But, as bad luck would have it, Mina fell ill a short time before. Though she was almost well enough on the day of the feast, she did not want to go.

"I shall not be lonely while you are gone, Papita, Mamita. I shall have Papagayo here to talk to." She held her finger out to her parrot which she loved well. She begged them to go, and they went off down the river in their canoe.

All would have been well, it may be, if the Indian had not forgotten to feed his snake that day. Anacondas can go many days without a meal, so he did not think it was important. In his haste to be on his way, Magu did not fetch the usual fresh meat out of his jungle traps for the snake.

And that day the giant snake was hungry. It crawled out of its dark corner, and its scaly head swayed this way and that looking for food. Possibly it was only because its stomach was empty. Or

147

perhaps it was really jealous of Mina who took up so much of the master's attention. Whatever the reason, its giant jaws opened wide. With one mighty gulp, it swallowed the girl.

Papagayo, the parrot, screamed when it saw what had taken place. It flapped its wings wildly and darted out of the hut door. Across the forest to the neighboring village it flew. There it circled among the merrymakers until it found Magu.

In those times animals talked. That parrot could say many, many more words than such birds today that only repeat what they have been taught.

"Master! Master!" the parrot squawked into the ear of the surprised Magu. "Master, come quickly! The snake has eaten poor Mina. It has swallowed her whole."

You may know that the man lost no time in getting back to his hut. He did not take his canoe up the river. Instead, he ran like a deer by a short cut through the woods.

There, beside the cooking fire, he found the anaconda asleep. And the Indian could see his child's slim form under the scaly skin of the big snake. Pacha-Mama, the Earth-Mother had taught these serpents strange habits. Having no teeth, they must swallow their food whole. And when their stomachs are full, they straightaway go to sleep.

"Boya! Boya!" the Indian father shouted the name by which he called his pet. "Wake, Boya! Give me my daughter again!"

But the snake did not stir. The only movement of its body was the struggles of the child, Mina, trying to get out again. Luckily there was enough air inside the anaconda's body so that she could still breathe. At least, that is how the tale is told.

Once more the man called, while the parrot screamed. But the creature would not wake up.

Then Magu made a plan. He brought in a freshly-killed paca from his traps, and he laid it on the ground close to the snake. He then heated a small stone until it was red hot and put it down nearby.

The smell of the freshly-killed paca, which the snake liked so well, made the sluggish creature lift up its head and open its eyes. The greedy serpent spread its jaws wide, as if to swallow the paca, and just at that moment, Magu threw the hot stone far down its open throat.

How that snake choked and coughed! It opened its burned throat so wide that it brought up the stone, and with it Magu's dear daughter.

Sometimes an anaconda squeezes its prey in its strong coils and thus breaks its bones before it gulps it down. Other times, like this one, it swallows an animal while it is still alive. Luckily that is what happened to Mina. The girl was able to breathe while she was inside the snake. And now when her father picked her up off the ground, she was unhurt.

Travelers tell fabulous tales about the giant snakes, like Magu's Boya, that live in the streams of the jungles along the Equator. Some say that these serpents are not long enough to swallow a child. But others remind them that this happened long, long ago. Perhaps it was in prehistoric times, when mammoths, including giant snakes, were on the earth.

The Indians of this part of Colombia say that its winding streams are the tracks left by such enormous serpents. They believe that when a lake is dried up, its serpent has gone away and will not come back again.

What became of the giant snake, Boya, in Magu's hut? The story does not say. But surely the Indian father would not risk his child's life a second time. Surely he told the anaconda to go away and never come back. No doubt the scar left in the snake's throat reminded it that its former master would have no pity upon it, if it did.

THE RING IN THE SEASHELL

IN SOUTH AMERICA ONCE—it could have been in Peru—there was a woman who had three grown sons. *Si,* three grown sons she had. But she had nothing else. Her husband was long dead, and like many another widow, this woman was poor. There were never enough silver pesos in her house to buy the few things she needed to keep herself fed and clothed.

Her three sons loved their mother. At least they always declared that they did. And one day the oldest one said to his brothers, "We must go out and find work. We must earn money to buy food and clothes for our poor mother."

"*Si, si,* my brothers," the second son agreed. "That is but our duty. We must go out into the world, and we must find work for which we shall be paid. Each of us must bring home at least a few pesos."

The names of the two older brothers do not really matter. The woman's youngest son was the important one, and he was called Nanco.

Now Nanco said nothing. He was one who liked to daydream. He liked to watch the birds and the butterflies. He liked also to

151

look out over the rolling waves of the sea. But he went along with the others. He thought perhaps he, too, could find work.

The two older sons of the poor widow sought work and found it. But Nanco just walked along the seashore and looked at the pretty shells and the round pebbles which the waves had rolled up there on the sands.

When the two older brothers brought home the silver pesos they had earned, the youth laid down beside them only a pretty pink shell which he had picked up on the beach.

His two brothers were angry.

"Who does not work, does not eat," they declared. They beat Nanco, and they drove him out of their mother's house. So, with his pretty pink seashell in his hand, the young man went sadly away.

Nanco walked far. By and by he felt hungry, and he looked inside his shell to see if it held anything good to eat, such as a snail or a clam. He was disappointed to find there was nothing there but sand. He was angry, and in a fit of temper, he threw the seashell down on the ground.

As the shell fell, however, Nanco saw the bright glint of silver in the sand which poured out of it. It was a ring, a bright silver ring, set with a yellow stone which gleamed in the sun. The young man made haste to pick up the ring, and to put it on his finger. He looked at it and looked at it, as if it bewitched him. Suddenly he felt drowsy, and he fell asleep by the side of the highway.

Voices woke Nanco. The sounds came from two rough-looking men who were riding together upon a big horse with a fine silver-trimmed saddle. The young man was frightened by their rude manners. But there was no place for him to hide. He was on an open plain.

"What are you doing here, boy?" one man asked him fiercely.

"I am only a poor youth looking for work," Nanco replied. And all at once he thought, what if they should try to take my silver ring from me? He turned the ring around on his finger, so that its shining yellow stone lay hidden inside his fist.

Then he heard one of the strangers say to the other, "Where did that boy go? A moment ago he was here. Now he is nowhere to be seen." They looked at one another.

Nanco did not understand what they could mean. He was there close beside them. "How is it they do not see me? Have they gone blind?" he asked himself. He walked closer. He reached for the silver-trimmed saddle. He lifted it from the horse's back and laid it down on the ground.

The two men were trembling when they set the saddle back on their horse.

"What can this be?" one cried out. "Who ever saw a saddle jump down off a horse's back all by itself?"

"They cannot see me even as I stand close to them," Nanco said to himself. "It must be that this silver ring has magic. It was when I turned its stone inside my fist, that I became invisible." And he stood very still as he listened to the words which the two men spoke to each other.

"Are we going mad?" one asked.

"Perhaps," said the other, "or perhaps this is the work of the Beast-with-the-Seven-Heads-and-Seven-Tails. Maybe he punishes us because we stole this sack of silver out of his cave."

Since they could not see him, it was easy for Nanco to creep closer. He gave each one of the two thieves such a sharp blow on the head that they fell, senseless, to the ground. Then he mounted

153

their fine horse with the silver-trimmed saddle.

The bag of silver pesos behind him was a heavy load for any animal but this horse was strong. He managed to carry it and Nanco too.

How the mother of this youth rejoiced when he poured the coins out on the table. Since they had come from the cave of the Beast-with-the-Seven-Heads-and-Seven-Tails, there seemed to be no reason why this poor family should not keep them and spend them. Everyone knew that the creature had stolen them himself when he raided their villages.

"You are too young to have so much money, Nanco," said one of his brothers. He was greedy, and he added, "Let me take care of it for you."

"You are not strong enough to ride such a fine horse. You had best give it to me." The other one also was jealous. And since they were both older and stronger than Nanco, they could easily have taken his treasures away.

Nanco, however, did not forget that he wore a magic ring on his finger. He jumped on the horse, and he turned the yellow stone around inside his fist. And when they no longer saw him, his brothers were frightened. Their eyes opened wide, their jaws dropped.

"What has become of Nanco?" cried one.

"The fine horse is gone, too, yet no one heard it gallop away!" They were more and more amazed as they thought about what had happened.

Not long afterward, one day when his brothers were not at home, Nanco came back again to see how it was with his dear mother. The woman was ashamed to face her youngest son. For his brothers had spent all her money. Not on goats or cows or useful things! Oh,

155

no, they had thrown their mother's silver pesos away on feasting and drinking, and betting on the horse races.

So Nanco lifted his mother up behind him on his horse. He rode away with her to a part of the country where the foolish brothers could not find her. There he bought her a house with the money he had kept for himself. She had all the food she could eat, and warm clothes to wear.

A horse is meant to be ridden. Nanco knew this, and day after day he rode over the land. One fine morning he came to a town on a hillside. There he found all the people sorrowful and afraid.

"It is because of the Beast-with-the-Seven-Heads-and-the-Seven-Tails," they told him. "He comes out of his cave in the rocks, and he carries off our young people, even our children. Many a brave youth has tried to kill this Beast-with-the-Seven-Heads-and-Seven-Tails. But none has ever returned."

Nanco himself was young and brave. He decided to try what he could do to rid these good people of their terrible curse. He rode his fine horse far up the mountain side until he came to the Beast's cave.

"Come forth, Beast," he shouted. "You with the Seven Heads and Seven Tails! Or I will come in after you."

There was a snarling and growling inside the cave. And the beast appeared. But before the creature could leap upon him, Nanco turned his magic ring around on his finger.

The Seven-Headed-One could not see the young horseman. It was quite easy for Nanco to keep out of reach while he cut off the Beast's seven heads and seven tails.

As the brave young hero stood looking down at the dead Beast, a wondrous thing happened. From each of the seven heads and from each of the seven tails there rose a young man and a young girl.

"Thanks to our deliverer! A thousand thanks!" they cried. "You came just in time. We were walking home from the meadows last night at dusk when we met the Beast. He swallowed us whole. Yes, you came just in time."

They begged Nanco to go with them back to their town so that they might make a feast for him. There, on the mountainside that rose above the sea, they sang and they danced. They ate and they drank and everyone rejoiced. Everyone, that is except one beautiful young girl who sat by herself, weeping. She would take no part in the gay merrymaking.

"Why are you sad, Sister?" Nanco asked gently. The girl was lovely to look at. His heart was touched by her tears.

"It is because the One-Legged Men have carried my father away," she explained. "Our land has another curse beside the Beast-with-the-Seven-Heads-and-the-Seven-Tails. This curse is the One-Legged Men who come in the dark of night when the moon does not shine. Their black boat makes no sound. And they seize any one who may be on the seashore. Many homes in this town are without fathers and sons because of the One-Legged Men."

"Let me see what I can do," Nanco said then. "Tonight there is no moon in the sky. I will place myself on the dark shore. We shall see what the One-Legged Men will do to me."

From his station on the beach, the young man at last saw a black boat glide through the darkness. It made no sound at all. It scarcely seemed to touch the dark water.

When the One-Legged Men jumped out of their boat and swam to the shore, Nanco pretended to sleep. He allowed himself to be taken and put into a sack and carried out to the black boat.

"We have brought a prize this time," these strange men said to their Captain. Proudly they opened their sack. But it was quite empty. Nanco had turned the yellow stone of his magic ring in towards his palm. So of course, he was invisible.

When the Captain saw no one inside the sack, he flew into a rage. In his anger he hopped up and down on his one leg. The sailors followed suit. It was all Nanco could do not to burst out into loud laughter at the sight of grown men hopping and hopping about on one foot.

While the sailors were trying to explain his disappearance, Nanco crept round their ship. A curious vessel, indeed, it was, this inky-black boat of the One-Legged Men. In the sea, all around it, there swam a throng of water-women; girls with long tails like those of huge fish. And in its hold the youth, Nanco, came on a great cage, filled with the poor village folk whom the One-Legged Men had carried away.

Meanwhile the sailors were searching their ship for the youth they had brought off the seashore. From top to bottom, from prow to stern, they sought their vanished prisoner.

"Well, he is not here," the Captain said at last. "We may as well have our dinner." So they ate and they drank. Then they went off to sleep.

Now Nanco seized a sharp axe, and he chopped off the heads of those One-Legged Men, one after the other. Since no one could see him he was able to catch them unaware.

The young man suspected that these were no everyday sailors. Of this he could be sure when he saw that red blood did not flow from their wounds. Instead there gushed forth black liquid which gave off a sickening odor.

158

"You are free now, my friends." Nanco unlocked the cage of the prisoners down in the hold of the ship. Out stepped the sons and the fathers of the sorrowing townspeople. Among them was the Chief whose beautiful daughter had so touched Nanco's heart with her tearful tale of woe.

Together, Nanco and the prisoners he had set free gathered up all the silver and gold they found on the ship. Together, they cut down its masts and let them float on the water. The men mounted the masts as though they were horses, and they rode them over the waves back to the safe seashore.

Only Nanco stayed behind. He set fire to the ugly black ship of the One-Legged Men. But since it was a demon ship, it never quite burned up. On dark nights, people say, the glow of its flames is still to be seen, far out on the sea to the west. No one dares go to put them out, for fear bad luck would come to him.

What about Nanco?

Well, there should be a bit of romance in every tale. And when Nanco swam ashore, the Chief's daughter greeted him with a wreath of bright flowers. She was so happy to have her dear father at home again that she gladly married the brave youth who had saved him from the evil One-Legged Men.

In time Nanco himself became the Chief of those people. But of all the riches he gathered, most precious to him was the magic silver ring with the yellow stone, which fell out of his seashell.

THE SAD, SORRY SISTER

IN THE LONG AGO TIMES, there dwelt in the deep forests of Argentina, an Indian youth and his only sister. The two lived alone in their little hut, for their father and their mother were dead.

The brother was the older. He was good-tempered and gentle, his words always were soft-spoken, and his manner was kind. The sister was different. She was unkind, and she delighted in tormenting her brother. In spite of her cruelty, the youth loved his sister. When she was scolding and cross, and so disagreeable that he could bear it no longer, he left her at her work of weaving a poncho and went forth from his hut.

I will go into the forest, he thought, where it is peaceful and quiet. I shall find more kindness among the beasts and the birds than I get here at home.

Then, as he wandered about in the woods, his good heart would soften. He would remember that she was his only sister and that he loved her. He would gather ripe fruit from the carob trees. Or he would find for her some wild figs, or the sweet honey which she liked above all other food.

Sometimes the brother brought home a young armadillo for the

160

cooking pot on their hearth. Sometimes he shot a fish with his bow and arrow, or perhaps even a fat turtle. He was good at hunting and fishing. And there was always food in their hut. Such a brave hunter he proved himself, no jaguar nor other fierce beast ever came within sight of his little home.

Small thanks he got from his surly sister for all the trouble he took to please her. The unfeeling girl never gave him a kind word. All he heard was complaints. She seemed to be pleased only when her good brother had a turn of bad luck.

There was the evening when he came home with his clothes torn to shreds.

"My sister," he pleaded, "today I had a bad fall from the top of a tree, which I had climbed to get honey for you for your supper. My clothes caught on its branches. Oh, they were sharp enough to make a jaguar weep. Would you be so kind as to sew up the holes in my shirt?"

But his hardhearted sister only laughed. "Sew them up for yourself," she cried. And she turned away.

Another day the brother returned with a deep wound in his back. "Dear sister," he begged, "Be kind, just this once! Wash my wound for me. A jaguar jumped out of the bushes upon me. I had no time to stop him with my hunting spear. Before I could kill the beast, his wicked claws tore this hole in my back. And I cannot reach it."

Again his cruel sister only laughed.

"Go wash it yourself in the river," she said. And she turned away.

So it went on, until at last the good brother's patience came to an end. It happened one afternoon when he had made his way home from the forest, weary and worn with a long day's hunt. Thirsty and tired, he threw himself down on his sleeping mat.

161

"Sister, O my sister," he cried, panting. "Give me some honey beer. Bring me a basin so that I may wash my tired, aching feet."

The cruel sister said nothing. She brought forth a gourd of the good honey drink and also a basin of pure cooling water, fresh from the brook. But instead of putting these down where her brother could reach them, she emptied them into the ashes on the hearth.

Her brother said nothing. But his gentle eyes flashed. Now, at last, anger was stirring in his loving heart.

Next morning, the girl lifted their manioc porridge off the cooking fire. But instead of serving her brother, she poured the good food out on the ground. Truly no one could imagine a sister so mean.

Again the young man gave no sign of his anger. But it was at this moment that his patience gave out. It was then he knew he could not live in the same hut with the girl any longer. It was then he decided what he would do.

A while later he called out, "Sister, today I go to the forest to climb a honey tree. High up in its trunk there is a hole which the bees have filled up to the top. They have laid so much honey in it that I cannot bring it all home by myself. Come along with me and help me to gather it."

As has been already told, this cruel sister liked honey. Better than anything else did she love this syrupy sweetness. So she agreed to go with her brother. It never entered her mind that he had not forgiven her for her wicked treatment this time, as he had always before.

She followed him along the narrow trail into the deep forest. The young man carried a long rope, "to help us climb high," he explained. He had also a sharp axe "lest we need to cut away branches from the honeybees' hiding place."

It was not long until they came to the tall tree. There it stood, like the very king of the forest, with its proud head seeming almost to touch the blue sky.

"I'll throw my rope over that high limb," the brother said to his sister. "I will climb the tree first. I'll pull you up with the rope. Then you can follow me from branch to branch until you reach the top where the honey is hidden.

"But go slowly! Speak gently! The bees do not like rough ways or harsh words. And the forest spirits will be angry if the bees are offended."

She was greedy for the promised feast of wild honey, so the sister climbed up the tree. All jungle folk in her part of the world, both men and women, knew how to set their bare feet against the rough bark of a tree trunk. This brother and sister went up and up.

"Higher now! Higher! The honey comb is still higher, Sister." So the youth urged the girl up into the very top of the tree. At last they came to the bee's nest. And bees were there in plenty.

The angry insects swarmed about the girl's head. They flew into her face until she cried out, "You'll have to gather the honey yourself, Brother. The bees are stinging me. I must cover my head." And she threw her poncho over her face, and waited safe in its shelter.

This was just as her angry brother had planned. He pretended now that he was taking the honey out of the tree. His sister had no thought that he might play a trick upon her. Her eyes were hidden under her poncho, so she did not see him climb noiselessly down from the treetop.

163

The bees buzzed about her ears with such noise that it was almost like thunder. So she did not hear the sound of her brother's sharp axe when he cut off all the lower limbs of that tree. Nor did she know when he picked up his rope and his axe and crept off down the trail.

After a time, the bees grew quiet once more. Now there was no sound at all in the forest.

"Brother! Brother!" the sister called softly so as not to stir up the bees again.

There was no answer.

"Brother, dear Brother!" she cried out again, this time more loudly. Again no answer came. Then the girl lifted her poncho so that she could peer out of its opening.

With a frightened cry she threw the poncho aside. She was alone. Alone in the top of the tall forest tree. And below her all the branches had been cut away so she dared not try to climb down.

Her head spun round and round when she looked at the ground so far below her. She grew dizzy with fear. She knew that she would fall to her death if her foot should slip. So she called again for her brother to come help her down.

Hour after hour she waited. Again and again she called out. But no one appeared. No sound broke the stillness. The sun set. The night fell. The sky grew dark, and no star pierced its darkness. Through all the long night, the sad sister sat there in the treetop, calling and calling.

"Brother! Brother!" she sobbed. "Where are you my brother? Always you have come when I have had need of you. Oh, my good, kind brother, forgive me. I truly am sorry I have treated you so badly."

Alas, the tree was so far away in the deep woods that the brother did not hear the pitiful cries of his sad, sorry sister. How then could he know that her hard heart had melted, and that at last she was sorry? He did not come.

All through the night the poor girl clung to the high tree branch, shivering in the chill of the south wind. Some forest spirit must have been moved by her cries for help. It must have looked deep down into her sad, sorry heart. For when morning came, the girl's feet which had clung so tightly to the tree branch had been turned into curving claws like those of a night owl. Her nose had taken on the shape of a bird's beak. And her two arms reaching out for her lost brother had become feathered wings. The Forest-god had taken pity upon her and turned her into a bird. In Argentina the name which people have given this bird is the *kakuy.*

Now in the form of a bird, the sad sister could easily fly down from her high prison. Now she no longer needed to fear the cold wind or the dark night. But she could not forget her dear brother and how badly she had repaid him for his early care of her. She opened her beak and she called for him again and again.

"Turay! Turay!" All through the night, and every night, the kakuy's pitiful cry rang across the green treetops. The Indians said its sound was the very same as their word for brother. Hunters still hear it when they spend the night out in the deep woods. Travelers whose way takes them out into the night are stirred by its sadness.

Everyone says that the kakuy's call, "Turay! Turay!" is the saddest cry in the world. All feel great pity when they listen to its sobbing notes. Even though she deserved her punishment, the tale of the sad, sorry sister touches their hearts.

THE-POT-THAT-COOKED-BY-ITSELF

A POT THAT COOKED by itself! Now there's something strange! Titu, the Indian who lived in the hot northern land of Guayana, thought so. He also thought it was a fine piece of luck when he came upon it.

Titu lived with his wife and his two sons in a hut on a river close to the Equator. Like many of his neighbors in that hot, humid land, this man did not like to work. The day was always too hot. At night one must sleep.

Now there really was not very much work for Titu to do. Even to build a new house in his land was not difficult. All that was needed was a roof of palm thatch set up on four posts.

It was his wife who took care of their patch of manioc plants. It was she who gathered the manioc roots, who grated them, and soaked them, and squeezed out their poison juice in her tipity. She dried their pulp, and she stirred it into coarse meal. And it was she who made the good manioc drinks and the porridge and cakes which supplied most of the family's food.

No, all Titu had to do was to hunt in the forest or fish in the river. His chief task was to bring home birds and game, turtles and fish so that there might be enough strength-giving stews in the family cooking pot.

167

But, lazy man that he was, he did not even want to do this. Like many another, he preferred to lie in his hammock and watch his wife work.

Often when Titu did go into the forest, he came home empty-handed. His arrows and spears failed to find their marks. Or else he did not trouble himself very much to shoot birds or to hunt for a peccary, the wild bush-hog his family liked so much to eat. Seldom did he find even a slow-moving turtle. His family often was hungry for a taste of good meat.

One day, when Titu was making his way through the thick jungle, he came to a little clearing in which there stood a small hut. Like his own, this one had a roof of dried palm leaves. It also had no walls, and only four slender posts held up its roof. So anyone who passed by could see all there was in it.

"Here is something strange," Titu thought. "Here is a hut. Here is a pot bubbling over a fire. Yet there's no woman to tend it."

He called out "Halloo!" But there was no answer. He called several more times. But the forest silence was unbroken.

Then Titu heard a voice. To his surprise it came out of the pot, bubbling over the fire.

"No one lives in this hut but me," said the pot. "Are you hungry, Good Stranger?"

"Why yes, I am hungry," Titu replied.

"What shall I cook for you, then? Shall it be a bird?"

"A bird, by all means." Titu stepped nearer. He peered into the pot. There, sure enough, a large fat bird was stewing. And when it was ready to eat, he thought it tasted better than any bird he ever had put into his mouth.

This is surely a lucky pot, a pot that cooks by itself, he thought.

169

"I shall tell no one about it. Alone I shall come here. There might not be enough to feed also my wife and my sons."

That night when the selfish man returned home, his wife came to meet him.

"Did you bring us some meat, Titu? Did you shoot us some birds?" she asked hopefully. Then, seeing him shake his head, she said "Oh, well, we still have some fish and some manioc cakes. Come, let us eat."

"I will eat nothing tonight. I am not hungry," Titu said carelessly. His wife wondered. Usually Titu ate more than anyone else. But she did not ask questions.

Next day, when her husband took up his bow, she called out, "May luck ride on your arrows! It is now many days since we have had in this hut anything to eat except a bit of fish and manioc porridge. Our sons grow weak, Titu. Try, oh, try hard to bring us some meat."

But instead of looking for game, lazy Titu made his way straight to the hut in the clearing. Again he found no woman tending the house. But again there was a fire and the lucky pot boiling above it.

"Good day," Titu said to The-Pot-That-Cooked-by-Itself. "Good day, Pot-That-Speaks."

"Good day, Stranger, are you hungry?" The pot's welcome words brought joy to the Indian.

"Ah, I'm very hungry."

"Well then, what shall I cook for you?"

"Cook me some meat. A stew of peccary will do very well."

"Good, that I will cook for you. But one thing you must know," the voice warned Titu, "you must take care, always, to leave something in the pot for another time."

170

The-Pot-That-Cooked-by-Itself boiled with great bubbles. Soon the man had under his fingers a fine meal of juicy bush-hog. He ate and he ate. The greedy man would have eaten every scrap of the meat, but he remembered the pot's warning. He left just a little stew on the pot's bottom.

"Did you bring us meat today, Titu?" his hungry wife cried. "Now, all we have is our manioc. No? Ah, well, here is your share."

"I do not want it. I am not hungry," the man spoke shortly. He lay down in his hammock and he went off to sleep.

So it happened each day. In the morning, the selfish man went into the jungle. At noon he feasted on the meat which the pot cooked for him. At night he came home empty-handed, and refused the poor fare which his wife set before him. His family wondered that he did not eat. But they wondered still more that he did not grow weak and thin.

"How can this be?" one of Titu's sons said to his brother. "Our father eats nothing here at home. Yet he is strong and well-fed?"

"Yes," said the other son, "there must be some trick. Let us follow him into the forest. Let us watch where he goes and what he does."

Next morning, when the man set forth with his hunting spear and his bow, the two boys crept after him. Like all jungle folk, they knew how to creep through the bushes without making a sound. Titu never guessed that they were behind him when he came to the strange hut with the blazing fire and bubbling pot.

"I'm hungry, O Pot," they heard their father say.

"What shall I cook for you, Titu?"

The boys' eyes opened wide with wonder. Could it be that this voice did come out of the pot?

171

Then they heard their father reply, "Today, I'd like monkey stew."

The boys could scarcely keep from crying out in their hunger when they smelled the good smell and saw the good food their father took from the pot. But they dared not show themselves.

Softly and silently, Titu's sons crept home. When they told their mother of the strange things they had seen and heard, the woman was angry.

"It is easy to see why your father does not want to eat our fish and our porridge. But we, too, shall feast from that Pot-That-Cooks-by-Itself. Try to remember each thing your father did. Try to recall what he said to the pot. We shall go there tomorrow while he fishes in the river."

The woman rose with the dawn. Before her husband could slip away into the forest, she laid out his fishing spear and the arrows he used to shoot fish in the river.

"Titu," she said firmly, "the manioc meal is almost gone. We must have fish for our supper or our children will starve. I will dig manioc roots. You must go get some fish."

The man could think of no excuse to refuse. He was not hungry, and one day without a visit to the hut in the clearing would do no harm. Though he did not really want to, he went to the river and set about spearing fish.

Meanwhile his sons led their mother through the jungle to the hut of The-Pot-That-Cooked-by-Itself.

"We are hungry, O Pot." The boys spoke just as they had heard their father speak the day before.

"What shall I cook for you?" The pot's reply was the same.

"Meat! Oh, cook us some meat! It is so long since we tasted meat,"

172

the hungry ones answered. And soon they were eating a great meal of peccary stew.

So hungry they were that they ate it up, every bit. Not one scrap of meat nor one drop of the broth was left in the pot. Why the pot did not give them the same warning it gave Titu, the tale does not tell. They even wiped the pot dry with the leaves off a fig tree.

That evening it was Titu's wife and his children who did not seem hungry for their supper of manioc and fish. But the man did not notice. He was too busy thinking how he could get away the next day to visit The-Pot-That-Cooked-by-Itself.

Somehow he managed it. Once more he made his way to the clearing. The magic pot was still there under its roof of thatch. But no fire burned beneath it. No savory steam filled the air.

"I am hungry, O Pot," the man said. "I will build you a fire. I will bring you fresh water for making good stew."

He brought the dry sticks, and he lit the fire. He filled the pot with brook water. But the pot did not say, "What shall I cook for you today?"

"I am hungry, O Pot," Titu said again. But again there was no answer. He grew sick with fear.

"Indeed, I am very hungry, O Pot. Will you not feed me today?" Then the voice answered.

"Your wife and your sons have been hungry for many days, Titu. I fed them all three yesterday. Why did you not bring them with you before, selfish man? I could have served them and you as well. Now you are punished for your great greediness. For even when they had eaten the meat I cooked for them, their hunger was not satisfied.

"They licked my sides clean. Not a scrap of meat nor a drop of

173

broth was there left for another time. You have broken my magic. Never more shall I be able to cook for those who pass my clearing.

"Go home, greedy Titu! Henceforth, if you want meat, you will have to get it for yourself."

THE HONEYBEE BRIDE

Tio was a honey-gatherer who lived in Guayana in the warm northern part of South America. He was lucky, that Tio. There was a time when he had more honey than he could eat. But like many another, he became careless and his good luck did not last.

In the long ago times, in his homeland there were honeybees everywhere. They made their nests in the trees, and they filled all the hollow places with sweet honeycomb. Every year, at the time of the honey harvest, the woods were thronged with men and women and girls and boys who came to get the sweet beefood. Sometimes they ate their honey in the comb. Or they stored it in great gourds called calabashes. Sometimes they also made it into the drink known as cassiri.

Tio was young. He was one of the best of the honey-gatherers in all the forest. He seemed to be able to find his way straight to the trees which the bees chose for hiding their sweet stores. The bees must have liked him, for he never was stung. And when evening came he had often more honey to take home than any of his friends.

But, like almost everyone, Tio grew weary of the work of gathering honeycomb.

"It's tiresome to walk and walk through the thick forest," he said

to himself. "I am worn out with climbing one tree after another in search of the bees. My arms ache with cutting open the hollow tree trunks where the comb hangs. Yet," he licked his lips, "nothing is so good as honey and cassiri."

One day when Tio was cutting into the trunk of a huge tree, he began to complain again.

"My arms are sore," he grumbled aloud. "If only there were a way to get honey without so much hard work. Yet honey—" The young man was just about to say that honey was well worth the trouble when a clear voice interrupted him.

"Take care, Tio. Hold your axe, or you'll hurt me." Out of the hollow tree rose the head of a beautiful Indian girl. And the young honey-gatherer fell back in his astonishment.

"Whoever are you? Where did you come from? How did you get inside this hollow tree?" The young man asked one question after another, and so quickly that the girl in the tree laughed.

"I am Maba, Sister-of-the-Honeybees. I heard you call my name. I live in this forest. I make my home in the hollow trees where honey is hid. It is I who help my brothers, the bees, to make the honey you take from us."

Tio was greatly struck by the bees' sister's beauty. If only I could persuade her to come live in my hut. What a fine wife she would be! She could show me the honey trees. What a life mine would be!

"Sweet Maba," he pleaded, "leave your home in the hollow tree. Come, dwell with me in my comfortable hut. You shall be my dear wife. You shall swing in a hammock while I do your bidding. How happy we could be!"

Now, the Sister-of-the-Honeybees knew well that she should not listen to Tio. He was a man, and men took their food away from the bees. But he was a fine young man, and it was dull in the deep woods. She would like to find out what life was like for the girls who lived in the houses of men.

"I have no proper clothes to wear in your hut." The Sister-of-the-Honeybees was a good deal like other girls. Her appearance was important to her. "I could not come to the world of men unless I had a white robe such as their women wear. Bring me some wild cotton. I will spin it into thread, and I will weave it into cloth. When I have made my white dress, I will come to live in your house."

Tio hurried away to a distant hillside where the wild cotton grew. He carried the fluffy white bolls to the foot of the honeybee maiden's tree. Perhaps the bees helped her. Or perhaps the forest spirits took a hand. But somehow or other, Maba spun the thread, wove the cloth, and made herself a robe so that she would look like any other Indian wife.

Tio was happy. He loved the Sister-of-the-Honeybees well. Life with her as his wife was indeed good. No longer did he have to walk through the deep woods in search of the honey he liked so well. The calabash in his hut was always full of its golden sweetness.

When Maba first came to her new home, she asked for a drink of the good honey beer called cassiri. Tio had made some for himself before she arrived. But with her first sip of this, the girl made a wry face.

"I do not blame you, dear Maba," Tio said. "It is but poor cassiri. It is pale, thin as water, and it has but little taste. I am not good at making cassiri. This is the best I can do."

"Fetch me a calabash full of fresh water," his bee-bride said then. She dipped her little finger into the clear water he brought her. Once, again, and a third time!

"Now try this, my Tio!" She poured a little out into a drinking gourd. The young man's face was bright with his pleasure. Never had he drunk cassiri as good as this.

"We must give a feast, Maba," he cried out in his delight. "The neighbors must taste the cassiri that fills my calabash now."

"*Si*, we shall give a feast, my dear husband." The Sister-of-the-Honeybees agreed. "But on one condition. No one must know who I am. You must give me your promise that you will not speak the name 'Maba' before our guests. It is our secret, that the Sister-of-the-Honeybees has come to live in the hut of a man. For my brothers would be angry. They would hide their nests far, far away in the forest, from the man who has taken their dear sister from them."

Well, the neighbors were invited to Tio's honey feast. The first day there came only a few. They had tasted the young man's cassiri before. They remembered how weak and pale it had been. The second day there were more guests. The word had spread that there was honey and cassiri in Tio's hut such as had never been eaten and drunk in that land before.

On the third and last day of the feast, so many came to eat and to drink that Tio was afraid his stores would not hold out.

"Do not fear, my Tio," his honeybee bride said, smiling. "Give to all who come. And give them all they can eat and drink."

Tio shook his head doubtfully. There was only one calabash of cassiri. But he obeyed Maba. He filled up one drinking gourd after another. Yet, always there seemed to be just as much honey beer in the calabash.

What a fine feast that was! The neighbors danced and sang. They ate honey, and they drank cassiri until the night fell.

179

Perhaps Tio himself drank a little too much honey beer. For he forgot how much he owed to his honeybee bride. In front of all their guests he spoke to her sharply. He ordered her to go here and to go there, to do this and to fetch that.

Then one of the guests picked up the calabash and tried to pour out another drink for himself. He tipped the huge gourd. He turned it upside down. Only a few drops dribbled into his cup.

"More cassiri here, wife!" Tio spoke roughly. And while his young bride took the calabash to the brook to fill it with water, the man began to boast about his good luck.

"Have no fear, my friends! There will soon be plenty of honey beer. My wife is no other than Maba, the Sister-of-the-Honeybees. She has only to dip her little finger in water to make more cassiri than we ever can drink."

Tio forgot his promise. He forgot his wife's warning that her name must be kept secret. Everyone stopped drinking to stare at the girl in the white cotton robe, who was now bringing the fresh water from the brook.

But Maba had heard Tio's careless speech. She gazed at him sadly. Then, while the guests watched, she set down the calabash and she flew up into the air.

Some said she had large wings, shaped like those of a honeybee. And it may well be she had. For she rose out of the clearing and was gone into the treetops before they could speak.

Tio ran after her. "Forgive me, dear wife! Forgive me! Come back! Oh, come back!" He called and called.

But the honeybee bride did not come back. She was lost amid the tall trees of the forest. And he never saw her again.

Gone was fair Maba, the Sister-of-the-Honeybees, from the hut

180

of Tio, the honey-gatherer. Gone, too, was his good luck. From that time on, the foolish young man had to trudge far through the deep forest in search of the bee trees.

It was as Maba had said. The bees hid their honey from him. He had to climb higher. He had to reach farther into the hollow tree trunks. And even when Tio, at last, found some wild honey, there was yet all the work of cleaning it and straining it and making his poor cassiri.

Well, these stories are ended
Like the Bee-Bride flown away.
But it may be you'll read them
Again, some other day.

NOTES

Page 11:

The Great Bird in the Carob Tree

Sources: *South American Sketches.* 1909, W. H. Hudson.
          Mes Montagnes. Joaquin Gonzales.
          Le Paysage et L'Ame Argentins. Aita et Vignale Ibarguren,
            1938.

In many parts of Argentina, the carob, or algarroba, tree was thought to be the dwelling place of gods and spirits. This evergreen tree grows to a great height; its roots go deep, as far as one hundred feet into the ground; its reddish pods have edible beans and a sweet pulp which is used for making flour and beer. The carob tree is so important that many Indians know it as "The Tree."

Its dried beans were once used as units of weight for precious metals and gems, whence the English word "carat."

Page 18:

The Crocodile's Daughter

Sources: *Mythology of all Races,* Vol. 11, *Latin America.* Hartley Burr
          Alexander, 1920.

This legend comes from the Carib Indians of Surinam. The Caribs, warlike and ferocious, cannibals in early times, are found in northern South America, and other Caribbean lands.

The cayman, mentioned in the story, is a large scaly species of crocodile, which may reach a length of 20 feet.

The calabash, the huge cannon-ball fruit of the calabash tree, grows big enough to enclose a man's head. Its hard, thin shell makes it a useful utensil for a jungle household.

Page 27:

The Youth Who Made Friends
With the Birds and the Beasts

Sources: *Myths of Mexico and Peru.* 1913, Lewis Spence.
　　　　Mythology of All Races, Vol. 11, *Latin America.* Hartley Burr
　　　　　Alexander, 1920.

This story was found in many parts of Peru. It comes from the
times of the Incas.

Page 36:

Jabuty, the Strong

Sources: *Amazonian Tortoise Myths.* Ch. Fred. Hartt, Rio de Janeiro,
　　　　　1875.
　　　　Brazil, and Legends of Brazil. H. H. Smith, 1879, 1880.

The jabuty is a small species of tortoise, common in Brazil, rel-
ished by both men and animals as food. Short-legged, slow, weak
and timid, the jabuty is the hero of many tales found along the
Amazon River, in which he is shown to be cunning and humorous,
and more clever than the other animals.

　　The Brazilian tapir, a water-hog, is brown, sturdy, and strong
but not very bright.

　　The whale in this story may have been simply a big fish, perhaps the piracuru, which weighs up to one-hundred pounds.

Page 43:

The Jabuty and the Jaguar

Sources: *Amazonian Tortoise Myths.* Ch. Fred. Hartt, 1875.
　　　　"Inquiry into Animism and Folklore of the Guiana Indians."

Walter E. Roth, *30th Annual Report, Bureau of American Ethnology, Smithsonian Institution,* 1908-1909.
Brazil, Legends of Brazil, H. H. Smith, 1879-1880.

This version of the tale comes from Guiana. The Indian name from which jaguar was taken means tiger. Unlike the striped tiger, however, this "tiger of Brazil" has a yellow coat, marked with black spots and rosettes. The largest of the American big cats, some jaguars have a length of seven feet.

Page 50:

A Trick That Failed

Sources: *Mythology of All Races,* Vol. 11. *Latin America.* Hartley Burr Alexander, 1920.
Myths of Mexico and Peru. Lewis Spence, 1913.

This nature myth comes from the Andean Indians in Peru.

Page 57:

The Gift of Manioc

Sources: *Brazil, the Amazons and the Coast.* H. H. Smith, 1880.
Folklore Brésilien. Frederico José de Santa-Anna Néry, 1889.

There are numerous other versions of the *Mani* legend. In one, the child who is buried is a boy. In another Mani was a man whose grave produced the useful plant. *Manioc* comes from *Mani-hot*, or House of *Mani*. Other names for the plant are *mandioca*, and *cassava*. From this sweet-potato-like root comes the bread and porridge of many South American tribes of Indians. Tapioca is also made from the *manioc* root.

Page 64:

The Golden Gourd

Source: *Folklore Brésilien*. Frederico José de Santa-Anna Néry, 1889.

Page 71:

The Little Black Book of Magic

Source: *Los Gauchos*. Juan Carlos Davalos, Buenos Aires, 1928.

The *gauchos* of the Argentine pampas were, in some ways, like the cowboys of the plains of the western United States. Their clothing, however, was different—loose and easy—baggy trousers tucked into their spurred boots, a shirt with full sleeves and a flowing tie, and a broad-brimmed soft hat. Their bolas, ropes for lassoing animals, were heavily weighted with stones or lead balls, attached to their ends.

Page 83:

Clever Carmelita

Source: *Folklore Chilien*. Georgette et Jacques Soustelle, Paris Institut International de Coopération Intellectuelle, 1938.

Page 93:

The Hairy Man from the Forest

Sources: *Brazil*. H. H. Smith, 1879, told him by Mario dos Rios, of Santarem.
Baron von Humboldt, who visited South America in 1803.
Mytho do Curupira. Ch. Fred. Hartt, 1875.

The *curupira* myth is found in many parts of South America, and the Spanish explorers reported it. Described as small, brown, hairy creatures, some people think the *curupiras* were a species of orangutan.

Page 100:

The Woman Tribe

Sources: *Brazil, the Amazons and the Coast.* H. H. Smith, 1879.
　　　　　Mythology of All Races, Vol. 11, *Latin America.* Hartley Burr Alexander, 1920.
　　　　　Numerous mentions of the Amazons are found, including those made by Columbus, Sir Walter Raleigh, and Baron von Humboldt.

In some versions, the lucky green Amazon stones were given only to the fathers of the girls born to the women.

Page 108:

The Beetle and the Paca

Sources: *Fairy Tales from Brazil.* Elsie Spicer Eells, 1917.
　　　　　Folklore Brésilien. Frederico José de Santa-Anna Néry, 1889.
　　　　　Mythology of All Races, Vol. 11, *Latin America.* Hartley Burr Alexander.

The emerald-green beetle has been made into bracelets and brooches and other ornaments. A thousand tiny points of gold shine on the green wings of the beetle, which is about as big as one's thumb nail.

The South American paca is a sturdy, ratlike creature about the size of a small rabbit. Its brown coat has a few pale spots, and it is eaten by animals as well as by men. It is noted for its speed in running. It resembles closely the ratlike agouty.

Page 115:

Children of the Sun

Sources: *Narratives of the Rites and Laws of the Yncas.* Sir Clements Robert Markham, Hakluyt Society, 1873.
Myths of the New World. Daniel G. Brinton, 1868.
Peruvian Antiquities. M. E. Rivero and J. J. Tschudi, 1868.
Myths of Mexico and Peru. Lewis Spence, 1913.

Page 123:

Golden Flower and the Three Warriors

Sources: Those cited under Children of the Sun and:
"Cuentos Andinos," E. Lopez Albujar, 1924, *Pan American Union Bulletin No. 70, Washington, D.C.*
Peru, Land of the Incas. E. George Squier, 1888.

Page 129:

The Magic Poncho

Sources: Those cited under Children of the Sun and:
The Incas of Peru. Sir Clements Robert Markham.

The poncho, a square sheet of cloth with a slit in its center for a head opening, was the chief mantle of the Indians and the *gauchos* in many parts of South America. Folded, it formed a saddle or a pillow. Open, it could be used as a blanket. Worn as a body covering, it would keep out cold and rain.

Page 137:

Mario and the Yara

Sources: *Folklore Brésilien*. Frederico José de Santa-Anna Néry, 1889.
Brazil. H. H. Smith, 1880.
Amazonian Tortoise Myths. Ch. Fred. Hartt, 1875.

Oiarais, the Indian name for water spirits, became *Yara* for the Portuguese settlers of Brazil. Some report they were mermaids with tails like porpoises. With their singing and dancing in the moonlight they enticed young men to their watery homes.

Page 144:

The Snake That Swallowed a Girl

Source: "Notes on the Eastern Group of Choco Indians in Colombia." Henry Wassen, 1927. *Journal of the Society of Americanists*, Paris.

Although cases of snakes swallowing children are frequently mentioned in South American folklore, doubts of their accuracy have been expressed. Smaller animals, however, have been found whole in their stomachs.

Page 151:

The Ring in the Seashell

Source: *Folklore Chilien*. Georgette et Jacques Soustelle, Institut International de Coopération Intellectuelle, 1938, told by Genoveva Oyarzun de Castro.

This tale is of Araucanian origin.

Page 160:

The Sad, Sorry Sister

Sources: *South American Sketches.* W. H. Hudson, 1909.
Le Paysage et L'Ame Argentins. Aita et Vignale Ibarguren,
1938.

Page 167:

The-Pot-That-Cooked-by-Itself

Source: "An Inquiry into the Animism and Folklore of the Guiana Indians." Walter E. Roth, *30th Annual Report of the Bureau
of American Ethnology, Smithsonian Institution, 1908-1909.*

This tale comes from the mythology of the Warrau Indians.

Page 175:

The Honeybee Bride

Source: "An Inquiry into the Animism and Folklore of the Guiana
Indians." Walter E. Roth, *30th Annual Report of the Bureau
of American Ethnology, Smithsonian Institution, 1908-1909.*

Some South American Names of People, Places, and Things and How to Pronounce Them

Allpa â′ē·pâ

Camila kâ·mē′lâ
Carlos kâr′los
Carmelita kâr·me·lē′tâ
Cavillaca kâ·vē·yâ′kâ
Chicha chē′châ
Coniraya ko·nē·râ′yâ
·Cori-Huayti ko′rē wâ′ē·tē
Curupira kū·rū·pē′râ
Cuzco kūs′ko

Floriana flo·ryâ′nâ

Gaucho gâ′ū·cho
Guanaco gwâ·nâ′ko

Huanuco wâ·nū′ko
Huathiacuri wâ·tyâ·kū′rē

Ica ē′kâ
Inca ēng′kâ
Inti ēn′tē

Jabuty jâ·bū·tē′
Jamundá jâ·mūn·dâ′
José ho·se′

Kakuy kâ·kwē′

Lino lē′no
Luis lwēs

Maba mâ′vâ
Maco mâ′ko
Magu mâ·gū′
Mama Oullo mâ′mâ o′ū·yo
Mamita mâ·mē′tâ
Mani mâ′nē
Mani-hot mâ′nē ot
Manioc mâ·nyok′
Manoel mâ·nū·el′
Manuel mâ·nwel′
Maramba mâ·râm′bâ
Maray mâ·râ′ē
Mario mâ′ryo
Mate mâ′te
Mina mē′nâ

Nanco nâng′ko
Niña nē′nyâ
Niño nē′nyo

Orellana o·re·yâ′nâ

Paca pâ′kâ
Pachacamac pâ′châ kâ′mâk
Pacha-Mama pâ′châ mâ′mâ
Pahy Tuna pâ′ē tū′nâ

Pampero pâm·pe′ro
Papagayo pâ·pâ·gâ′yo
Paricaca pâ·rē·kâ′kâ
Paucar pâū·kâr′
Paucarbamba pâū·kâr·vâm′bâ
Pedro pe′thro
Peso pe′so
Pillco-Rumi pē′ē·ko rrū′mē

Rancho rrân′cho
Rondos rron′dos
Runtus rrūn′tūs

Sapa Ñusta sâ′pâ nyūs′tâ
Señor se′nyor
Señorita se·nyo·rē′tâ

Silverio sēl·ve′ryo

Tanca tâng′kâ
Tata tâ′tâ
Teresa te·re′sâ
Tio tē′o
Tipity tē·pē·tē′
Titicaca tē·tē·kâ′kâ
Titu tē′tū
Tomaso to·mâ′so
Tópac to′pâk
Turay tū·râ′ē

Upar ū·pâr′

Yara yâ′râ

Pronunciation symbols are taken from THE FOLLETT WORLD-WIDE SPANISH DICTIONARY, © 1966.

KEY TO THE SYMBOLS: â *as in* father; e *as in* ate; ē *as in* be; o *as in* go; ū *as in* too; consonant symbols approximately the same as English except for r (slightly trilled), rr (strongly trilled), and v (midway between English b and v).

Frances Carpenter

As the daughter of Frank Carpenter, himself a well-known writer, Frances Carpenter (Mrs. W. Chapin Huntington) has always been close to the literary world. She wrote her first book at the age of ten. Later, she and her father collaborated on three juvenile books.

After graduation from Smith College, she married W. Chapin Huntington, a foreign service officer who was also a writer.

Frances Carpenter has written more than thirty books, many of them dealing with folklore. She has also published historical fiction and a number of elementary school geography textbooks.

When not on one of her many expeditions to gather material for new books, she lives in Washington, D.C.

Ralph Creasman studied at the Art Institute of Chicago, Peabody College, Nashville, and the New School for Social Research. His work has appeared in national magazines, and he has illustrated several children's books. Mr. Creasman, a Chicago free-lance artist, divides his time between his art work and research on primitive cultures.